THE WOLF WHO PLAYED WITH FIRE

CRY WOLF
BOOK THREE

SARAH MAKELA

KISSA PRESS LLC

THE WOLF WHO PLAYED WITH FIRE

CRY WOLF, BOOK 3

Some magic can't be unspun...

Meddling in magic...

If Mia Brooks could turn back time, it would be to when she used her fledgling magic to craft a potion for an injured werewolf. It nearly killed the Pack Alpha, and now the lives of her witch mentor, Jessa, and her soldier boyfriend, Ethan Parker, have been changed forever. Jessa is in hospital after a vicious werewolf attack. And, Ethan, having being bitten, is becoming a werewolf himself.

A wolf at the door...

Mia can't turn back time, but she can try to make things right with the two people she cares about most. She's keeping Jessa's shop, Eternally Magick, open, and she's there for Ethan as his inner wolf grows. But, by the next full moon, his transformation will be complete. Can she really be the mate of a half-man-half-wolf, living within the law of the Pack?

Under his spell...

Struggling to contain his new lupine senses, Ethan goes missing on active duty. When Mia realizes her werewolf lover has been abducted, she knows must harness every magic power she possesses to get him safely back...

The Wolf Who Played With Fire

Editor: Tessa Shapcott

Cover Artist: The Killion Group

ISBN-13: 978-0-9910469-4-2

MIA

*W*ater slid over my body, and I lifted my face to the warm spray. Delicious soreness ached in my muscles as I reached for the shampoo. Crashing at Ethan's house was dangerous, but the romantic rendezvous we'd shared had taken me to new heights of pleasure.

However, not all good things last forever.

My brother, Nolan, lived with Ethan, keeping an eye on the place while Ethan was deployed with the Army. Neither of us knew exactly when Nolan would arrive home from spending the weekend with his girlfriend, but he had work in a few hours. The chances of him swinging by were high. That meant I needed to leave as soon as possible.

Part of me hoped I could slink away before Ethan woke up, but it was only a matter of time before he stirred. The fact he hadn't yet indicated to me just how 'active' we'd been last night, since not only was Ethan a trained soldier, but now he was becoming more and more of a werewolf. That last part scared me.

I leaned my forehead against the white tiled wall. Regret squeezed my heart like a vise. It would be so easy to blame

Jessa, my friend and mentor, for pushing me into the werewolf debacle, and even easier to torment myself for having used wolf's bane. If I'd gone with the common method of crafting the salve instead of making my own potent blend, then this would not have happened.

Those thoughts led to madness. I balled my hands into fists. Neither Jessa nor I could've known what was going on.

The supernatural world was one of magic and potions. Witches were real since I was one. Werewolves, on the other hand, were beasts of legend, not fact. That shocking revelation brought fear and pain crashing through my door and harmed those I cared about.

Both Ethan's and Jessa's lives were changed forever, because I couldn't protect either of them from the werewolf's attacks. The ramifications of my failure were incomprehensible, especially for Ethan.

Releasing a sigh, I focused on the bar of soap and reached within myself for my magic. Jessa made telekinesis appear so effortless. If I'd learned one thing recently, it was that I kept myself locked away, hoping others wouldn't burn me at the stake. Being powerless wouldn't help those I cared about, or me, when the time came to protect them.

Fear and atrophy shriveled my magical muscles. While I still wasn't convinced about using my power, especially not as openly as Jessa did, I refused to wait for the next disaster to hit before I acted. Something deep inside me knew we weren't out of the woods yet.

No matter how hard I concentrated, the soap remained rooted in place. Ugh.

How could I measure up as a witch if I couldn't even accomplish the basics? If my grandmother were here, life would be much easier. Instead, she rested in her grave.

The bathroom door creaked open and my heart leapt into my throat. Panic pushed me to remain small and silent, even though the spraying warm water gave away my presence. If Nolan was home before work, I would be screwed.

My brain scrambled for excuses about why I was here, much less why I was taking a shower.

The mugging wouldn't work anymore. Things had mostly gone back to normal. I spent more time at home whipping up potions for Jessa's new age shop, Eternally Magick.

With Jessa in the hospital, she couldn't run the shop, and I needed to help. What family she had was several states away, and they couldn't or wouldn't take time from their lives to assist her.

Besides, Ethan and I didn't need to be as careful about Nolan coming around to my place. He rarely swung by these days, and when he did, he usually called first.

"Mia? Everything okay in there?" Ethan nudged back the shower curtain, tension tight in his naked shoulders.

Air whooshed from my lungs in a rush and my shoulders slumped forward in relief. "You scared me."

"Sorry, sweetheart. I felt a lot of energy buzzing in here. Just wanted to make sure you're okay." He let go of the curtain, and it fell back into place. The slightest twinge of sadness nibbled at me, but this was for the best. If he got in the shower with me, I might never leave.

"It's okay. I was just—" Wait. Would telling him the truth about my attempt at telekinesis be a good idea? He might laugh. "I got caught up in my thoughts. I have to be at Eternally Magick in an hour, and I'll probably stop by the hospital later to talk to Jessa. I won't be home until late."

Ethan had attended a couple Pack meetings in the past few weeks, but I'd never asked for more details. If he wanted to share what he'd learned, he would tell me. However, I couldn't wait around forever, I needed to know... "Do you know anything about the werewolf who attacked us and nearly killed Jessa?"

A long pause swept through the bathroom, and for a moment, I didn't think he'd answer.

"His name is Jared Grant." Ethan's voice was close as if he stood inches from the white and blue shower curtain, hovering just out of sight. "He was the Pack's second in command. The role changed to the Alpha's son, Chad, who has been sticking true to his word. He's helping the Pack come onboard with the idea of me joining them." He let out a sharp hissing sigh. "A few of the members weren't sure I should live, since it's against the Alpha's wishes for new wolves to be made. Chad convinced his father I would make a good addition."

Strength drained from my body. I had no idea they would've killed him. "God, Ethan." I braced myself against the tiled wall, uncertain if my legs would hold under the weight of that revelation. "You should've talked to me. H-how could I have helped to stop them if they'd tried to... kill you?" Nausea bubbled within my stomach and I wrapped an arm under my breasts, cradling my belly. An urge to puke lingered at the back of my throat.

The shower curtain jerked open, and Ethan leveled his gaze at me.

My heart skipped a beat and my foot slid on the wet tub. I tumbled forward, the fall happening in eerily slow motion.

Ethan caught me and pulled me against his solid chest. "Careful." He kept a steady grip on me as I regained my shaky balance. "There are dozens of werewolves in the Pack. How do you expect to cause much damage?"

His words stung. Even though I wanted to be defensive and lash out, he was right.

While I tried to convince myself I was some badass witch capable of raining down chaos on the werewolves, that wasn't me. They would squish me like a bug under their feet, especially since wolves worked together.

I pushed past Ethan and grabbed a towel. Standing naked before him had lost its appeal. Maybe if I hadn't tried telekinesis and gotten so emotional, we wouldn't be having this conversation.

"Come on, babe. Don't pull away." He grabbed my hips, turning me around to face him. "I don't want you to get hurt, okay? Not after the close call in the parking garage. Plus, your friend is in the hospital because of a werewolf. I don't trust the Pack, and they don't trust you after you nearly killed their Alpha."

A shiver chased across my spine that was only partly due to the air's coolness. "I don't want you hurt either," I said, forcing myself to meet his gaze. "I'm willing to risk my safety for yours."

The gentle touch of his warm hands shifted, and his fingers bit into my skin. "Mia, I can take care of myself. It's you I'm worried about."

Through the heat of his words, a sting of power and desire set me alight. The sensation dimly reminded me of what I'd felt when Mr. Sexy...er...Jared...had touched me in Jessa's shop.

Planting my palms on Ethan's chest, I refused to let those memories take hold of me, except the feel of my palms on his hard chest melted my insides and made me pliant and willing. My body wanted Ethan more than it wanted its next breath.

Ethan stared into my eyes transfixed. He bent for a kiss, and any desire I had to keep my distance evaporated as our lips met. Lust crashed through me, and my only need was to be intimate with him. Within seconds, he propped me on the bathroom counter. His hands slid down to my knees before he made his way back toward my naked thighs.

Passion warmed me, taking away any chill I'd felt, and I

parted my legs, anxious to be one with him. "Ethan, I want you inside me."

Whatever negativity from the argument vanished like waking from a bad dream. The only importance now was getting his boxers down and rolling a condom on him. Did he have any in here? Because I didn't know if I could wait until we reached his room.

He parted my towel and tugged me closer. My backside dangled rather precariously over the counter's edge, but he wouldn't let me fall. Despite, or maybe because of, all we'd been through, I trusted him. He looked out for both our relationship and for me.

Wetness formed between my legs at the fierce hunger in the way he claimed my mouth. His tongue speared me, brushing along mine with a need to possess. He slid his hand between my legs, teasingly trailing it over my lips.

I wrapped my arms around his neck and he gripped my hips, lifting me into his arms. Apparently, we were headed to the bedroom. The press of his hot erection between my thighs as he adjusted my position sent heat through me like a wildfire.

For a moment, I didn't care we had responsibilities outside of these four walls. If he asked me to spend the day with him in bed, I would do it.

Ethan strode toward the door with the towel forgotten on the bathroom counter. As we approached the exit, he sucked in a breath and froze.

Loud banging on the bathroom door nearly made me scream, but I slapped a hand over my mouth. If it wasn't for Ethan's warning, I might have blown it.

He set me to my feet then blocked the door with his muscular frame. The muscles in his back twitched with barely contained aggression.

"I have to use the restroom, man." Nolan knocked again, a

little more impatient this time. "Showers can be a luxury when deployed, but come on. I have to leave for work soon." Humor was evident in his voice, but their relationship wasn't as strong as it had been. Was I the cause of their problems?

"Sure, just a moment," Ethan said. He ducked his head under the shower's spray that both of us had ignored in our burning lust then shut off the water. He wrapped my towel around me, motioning toward the shower.

I opened my mouth to argue, but his severe frown had me shaking my head in defeat. With a huff, I gathered my clothes.

Water dripped down Ethan's chest and my mouth watered, wanting to slide my tongue over his skin. The moment passed as he grabbed a towel.

Before I closed the shower curtain, I mouthed 'you owe me' to Ethan, who managed to suppress a chuckle. The sparkle in his eyes was more than enough to make me wish Nolan hadn't interrupted us. The doorknob rattled a little as Ethan turned it.

My brother stomped into the bathroom. "You sure took your time," Nolan grumbled, his shadow pausing near the sink. "Did you get a new purple hairbrush for your thick, flowing hair?" I balled my hands into fists. Shit! I knew I'd forgotten something. "Wait. This looks like Mia's. What is it doing here?" The soft clap of plastic on marble indicated he'd set it back on the counter.

"Huh, I didn't notice. Maybe she forgot her brush when she last stayed over?" Ethan flung his towel over the curtain rail, leaving it to dry and giving me a little more concealment.

"Must have." My brother sounded a little confused, but he let it go. "I'll give her a call later. She really hates when her stuff goes missing. But, seriously, I have to go."

A sharp slap of energy sizzled from Ethan, conveying his

emotions more than any words could, but he left. His control was slowly unwinding. Time would tell if he'd be able to keep calm as a werewolf, even when others pressed him.

For now, my immediate concern was staying hidden from Nolan. When we were kids, I'd sucked at hide and seek. He had possessed an almost superhuman ability to find me, no matter where I'd hidden. I only hoped that superpower had faded with time.

The one thing separating Nolan and me was the thin shower curtain. Thankfully, you couldn't see through it, but I hated being stuck in here. If he looked behind the curtain and saw me wrapped in a towel, he'd know what was going on between Ethan and me.

After the celebration with my family on Christmas Day, I trusted Ethan knew what he was talking about. Neither my parents nor my brother needed to know about our relationship, not yet at least. We could explore each other and see if we worked first, especially with Ethan's upcoming transformation. Part of me wasn't sure I could handle him as a werewolf.

Stop overthinking it.

If I could fight Jared as a novice witch, then surely I could work through my issues with the wolves. Chad, the Alpha's son, had been okay once we'd figured out who the real villain was. Unfortunately, it didn't seem like the rest of his Pack agreed.

The toilet lid smacked the back of the commode, and I bit my lower lip. My stomach churned and nausea swirled through me anew. Everything within me prayed that Nolan took a leak and not anything else. Silence would be hard won if he did more.

The loud unzipping of his pants shot panic through me. If my brother sat, I'd lose my nerves. Scanning the shower, I looked for some way out that wouldn't end with me being seen, but there was no escape.

A steady stream of urine and the following flush of the toilet nearly had me sighing in relief. He washed his hands, brushed his teeth with an electric toothbrush and fixed his hair for what felt like hours. I had no idea my brother was this meticulous with his morning routine, when he looked like he'd barely rolled out of bed most days.

Closing my eyes, I stayed as quiet as I could. Silence filled the air, then the shower curtain crinkled a little as it moved. I snapped my eyes open, a scream building in my throat.

"Hmm... There should be more moisture in his towel." The gig was up. Any minute now, he'd open the curtain. I was toast.

The loud blare of rock music shrilled through the bathroom, and Nolan groaned a second before answering his phone. "Hey, sexy, I was just thinking about you. What? Your car won't start? Did you try getting a jump?" He laughed at something his newest girlfriend said, probably a dirty joke. "Sure, I can take you. Let me finish up at home first. I'll see you soon."

The bathroom door opened then snapped closed. Oh God, that was too close.

Waiting a full minute before acting, I carefully moved the damp curtain enough to confirm what I'd heard. Nolan was gone. *Good.* However, he could come back. If I didn't go now, I might be giving away the chance to leave undetected.

I couldn't repeat this stressful situation. I had to get out.

Slipping into my clothes, I remained quiet like my life depended on it. My ears strained to hear any movement in the hallway. Once dressed, I climbed out of the shower and hung my towel inside in case Nolan came back.

The blinds were drawn at the bathroom's small window. While we were on the second floor, I didn't have many other options. The last thing I wanted was for the boys to fight. With Ethan slowly transforming into a werewolf, I wasn't sure how much control he had now, especially with the incredible wave of power he'd given off earlier. Besides, my family wouldn't understand us. Most of the time, they didn't even get me.

I reached beneath the blinds to unlatch the window. My attention was still focused on my surroundings. If the door opened now, anyone could see me. The window squeaked as I lifted it. The blinds could remain lowered if I could slip outside without wasting more time.

Glancing back at the sink, I thought about taking my hairbrush with me. However, that would be a surefire sign of my presence. It was better for Nolan to think I'd forgotten it, even if I suspected he didn't totally buy Ethan's excuse.

Pulling myself through the window presented a problem. It was positioned on the wall at chest height. Fortunately, the toilet was nearby.

There was no way around it. I pulled up the blinds, then used the toilet lid to climb out the window, legs first. Sitting on the windowsill, I plotted how to drop without hurting myself. Fear clenched my chest. The distance to the ground was bigger than I'd anticipated. Some say they're afraid of heights, but heights aren't my problem; it's falling.

What had I been thinking? I started to drag my legs back into the bathroom and wait in the shower for Nolan to leave, but footsteps in the hallway steeled my resolve.

Wind rushed through my hair and I bit back a scream as the ground flew up to greet me. My feet hit first, but the momentum threw me to the right. The pleasurable ache Ethan had lit within my body snapped into searing pain.

I sank my teeth into my lower lip, looking up at the bathroom window. Thankfully, no one stared back.

Climbing to my feet was a burden. My right ankle badly

hurt, but nothing appeared broken. I'd make a comfrey poultice when I arrived home. Still, I could support some of my weight without bringing too many tears to my eyes.

With one last backward glance, I quickly limped through the backyard of Ethan's neighbor. This way I could cut cross over to the next street and hobble home without Nolan spotting me. My bare foot squished on something wet, and I glared at the sky. I had just taken a shower. This was not so fair.

The Universe had to be picking on me. Mornings couldn't possibly start this wrong without help.

2

ETHAN

*W*ith each passing minute, my anxiety increased. Was Mia okay? Nolan had suspicions about her hairbrush being there, and I only hoped he didn't act on them and find her hiding. That would raise questions better kept secret for now. With everything going on in the Pack, I didn't need more stress.

I hovered in the doorway to my bedroom, keeping my ears open for any sign of Nolan leaving the restroom. With how good my hearing was these days I could've been further away, but concern refused to let me get that comfortable.

Then again, my improved senses hadn't helped me detect Nolan's presence in the first place. Somehow, Mia overrode them all. Being intimate with her had been my top priority. My cock was still half-erect from our close encounter. A cold shower would be in my immediate future.

My job resumed soon. Who knew how that would go? With what had happened with Mia during Christmas break, and my future as a werewolf, my career wasn't exactly top priority, but I'd used up my leave. Maybe getting out of the house would do me good.

The door opened to the bathroom and I tracked Nolan's footsteps as he headed down the hall. *Damn.* I hated walking on eggshells with him, but our friendship had been tense since Christmas Day. He hadn't liked that I didn't come home on Christmas Eve. But I'd been in bed with Mia after the fight in her friend's shop and ensuing hospital visit.

He thought I was hiding something, which granted I was, but the cold shoulder frustrated me to no end. I'd spent a year of my life overseas thinking about how good it would be when I came home, but my life was turning upside down.

Anger flowed through me stirring my beast, and I squeezed my hands into fists until the joints in my fingers hurt. Each moment that passed, my wolf grew stronger and more dominant. If I didn't calm down, he might take over. The last thing I needed was to explain to Mia why I'd mauled her brother.

I crossed the span of my room to rummage in my closet. He might ask fewer questions if he thought I was busy, or at least I hoped so.

Instead of him coming in, he walked by. Should I be relieved or worried? This could be the end of our lifelong friendship.

The door to his bedroom shut and I walked to the hallway, checking to see if the coast was clear. It was.

I stalked down the hallway then slipped into the bathroom, but I came up short as I saw the open window. *What the hell?*

The blinds bumped against the windowsill as a breeze cooled my skin. Did Nolan open the window? He'd never done so before.

Mia? She could seriously hurt herself. Sucking in a deep breath, I noticed her scent was fainter than it should've been. My feet carried me toward the window. Mia half-jogged, half-limped away barefooted. Damn. Her shoes were still in my bedroom. I needed to hide them in case Nolan snuck into my space while I was gone later.

The muscles in my jaw tightened, but I forced myself to keep my cool. Part of me wanted to run after her and make sure she was okay. I couldn't. We both had things to do.

The last thing we needed was more tension in our lives. She was helping her friend, even though her parents weren't happy their daughter was caught up in 'magical mischief.' I was coping with the aftermath of the werewolf attack, not to mention the stuff I'd been through overseas while deployed. Some nights I tossed and turned, but when Mia was beside me, I slept so much better.

I walked to the shower, then pulled back the curtain. The towel she'd been wrapped in hung on a towel rack. Her lingering scent spread heat through my groin. Desire to rub the soft terry cloth against my cheek and bask in her scent dredged up uneasiness in me. Already my urge to protect her was a wild and fierce thing growing not by days, but by hours and minutes.

My humanity slowly faded. Would I still be the man Mia fell in love with? Time would tell.

Nolan paused in the doorway of the bathroom. He glanced between the open window and me staring into the shower. Thankfully, I'd released the towel in time. "Dude, I thought you already took a shower. Might not be a good idea to have the window open if you're taking another one. It's January. You'll catch a cold."

Somehow catching a cold didn't seem to be the worst of my problems these days. I chuckled. "No, I'm not taking a shower. I'm airing out the room while I clean. The ventilation isn't as good as it could be."

He shrugged. "Take it easy. Tonight's poker with the guys, remember?"

"Yep, I'll be here. Don't forget the beer." I had forgotten, but with Mia looking after her friend, I'd be available. I hated the nights we had to sleep in separate beds, but it was just how things would be until something changed.

Grinning, Nolan released a held breath. "Will do." He waved then darted out of sight, his footsteps retreating downstairs.

Frustration grated in me. I snatched up the towel Mia had used. Before I knew what I was doing, I ripped it in half. The fabric limply dangled in my hands and I tossed scraps to the floor. I'd always prided myself on loyalty, trust, and honor. Yet what I was doing with Mia betrayed all of that.

My friendship with Nolan hung in the balance, waiting for me to make a decision that would either repair our bond or forever destroy it. I leaned against the window, but Mia was long gone now.

No matter what I did, I could lose them both.

3

MIA

*W*hile Jessa was in the hospital, I helped at Eternally Magick. She didn't have a lot left over to pay me with after shop expenses, especially now that she had medical bills. What she could give me helped with gas and groceries. My work here made me hesitant to ask my parents for any help.

Their hopes about the 'Wiccan stuff' being a fad grew more distant. But I knew the truth. I came from several generations of witches, but my parents had no clue. My grandmother had known my mother didn't have magical power, so she'd never shared that part of herself with her daughter. When I was old enough to understand, she'd begun teaching me what she knew.

However, she'd died far too soon. I had so little knowledge about the purpose of my powers and how to use them. Her death had been mysterious, but everyone explained it away as a freak accident.

That's when I'd met Jessa.

Some friends of my grandmother had directed her into

my path. If it weren't for Jessa, I'd still be floundering like a fish out of water.

Sitting behind the shop's counter, it took all my strength to keep from laying my head against the display case's cool glass. The delicious evening with Ethan had worn me out, and now pain radiated from my ankle. The jump had hurt far more than I'd realized.

Besides, it wasn't every day that I threw myself from the window of a second story building. By the time I got home, I'd had to clean my feet and go. After work, I would make the comfrey poultice for my ankle. I doubted it was broken, but I'd definitely strained it.

However, I couldn't believe Nolan had stomped in like that. He'd changed since the argument between him and Ethan on Christmas Day.

I didn't like seeing their friendship slowly deteriorate, especially when I was causing those problems. If our relationship cost Ethan and Nolan their friendship, then I didn't think I could handle being with Ethan, even if I wanted him more than I'd ever wanted anything else.

The book on werewolves I'd found in Jessa's office sat on the counter near me. While I'd done some research, I wondered what I'd find if I did more digging. The wolves I'd met scared me. Knowing Ethan would become one of them made it that much worse. Should I learn the grim details of how he'd be, once the transformation to werewolf was complete?

Reluctantly, I held my hand over the book, focusing my energy on it and willing the text to show me something happy. I flipped it open, letting the pages reveal what I was supposed to see. The page it landed on had no pictures, and I breathed a sigh of relief. The yellowing paper flipped of its own accord, revealing an illustration of a 'wolfman' biting into a small person, maybe a child.

Violence, *horror* and *torn to pieces* were the first words that captured my attention. I ran a hand through my hair. No, I wouldn't go by superstition as the basis of whether or not I should spend my life with Ethan.

A cool draft blew through the shop. Shivering, I wished I hadn't left my jacket in Jessa's office.

I shut the book again, then reopened it closer to the beginning, determined to read more about werewolves and conquer my fears. I'd learned my lesson, and I refused to backslide when I knew how much it had cost the ones I loved.

The more I read, the more nausea plagued me. Maybe this explained why Jessa hadn't told me much about werewolves. Geez... Sure, I'd believed her when she said she didn't know if they actually existed, but she had the book in her office. It wasn't as if she didn't know anything at all.

I shoved the old leather bound tome to my left. Now wasn't the time to get this heavy and upset about what was happening in my life. If an actual customer walked in, I didn't want to be surly and on the verge of tears.

Happy thoughts. That's what I needed. Memories of our nearly shared intimacy this morning drifted through my head. Ethan was the only one who truly accepted me for who I was. Everyone else in my life tried to change me or wanted something from me—even Jessa—although most of them had the best intentions. But being loved by Ethan was like the cure I'd been waiting for.

Maybe if I straightened a few of the shelves, I wouldn't be quite so emotional or exhausted. Then again, my foot still hurt, and I was under no illusions of my feelings changing course. I laid my head on the counter seconds before the bell that was connected to the door chimed.

Darting upright, I pretended I hadn't been about to take a

nap. That was the last thing I needed, especially since quite a few of the customers knew Jessa personally. They would probably tell her if I did something wrong like sleep on the job. Plus, if an unsavory type came in and stole something... I'd rather avoid that.

Nevertheless, taking over for her put me in front of many people, some of whom I wished I'd never met. The energy they poured out was overwhelming, like trying to breathe water. How could I stack up without my grandmother's guidance? Jessa did the best she could, but it was far from what I needed to succeed.

Maybe she was holding back. After all we'd been through a few weeks ago, I wondered if she'd open up to me now. The hospital visits didn't reveal much. We talked about the store and life in general. The type of conversation a couple of friends would enjoy, not a novice witch to her mentor.

Dread slithered down my spine as I glanced up at the man who had walked into the shop. Chad looked every bit as arrogant as when he'd broken into my house and almost punched me in the head after I'd inadvertently poisoned his father and Alpha. Fortunately for me, he'd needed my help.

I'd crafted him a potion and cast a few high-powered fireballs at Jared to keep him from ruining more of Jessa's shop. Chad hadn't liked my interference, but the bastard had hurt my best friend.

The energy buzzing around Chad was wild and angry. This was the first time I'd seen him since our prior meeting, but I knew Ethan interacted with him since they went to Pack meetings together see if he was worthy to be one of them. The fact they'd nearly killed Ethan because he'd been made into a werewolf without permission terrified me.

"What do you want?" I asked, pushing myself to my feet. I didn't want to be taken off guard if he made a move for me.

"Nice to see you again too." Chad's voice was dark and mocking. "Do you greet all of your customers that way?" He glanced around the shop as if inspecting it for the first time. Or maybe he was seeing how well I'd cleaned it up since he and Jared had nearly destroyed it.

"No, but most of them are here to buy things, not intimidate me." I remained behind the counter, remembering how quick he was. My heart raced in my chest, and I took a couple deep breaths to try calming down. If he knew how badly he was bothering me, it would give him more power over me.

"If I was trying to intimidate you, you would know it." He walked over to the counter, taking his time looking at the statues and magical paraphernalia he passed.

"That doesn't answer my question." I pulled air into my lungs steadily, willing myself to breathe and act as if he didn't unnerve me. "I know your people don't like me, but I didn't poison your Alpha intentionally, as you already know." He narrowed his eyes at me. "Besides, what have you done to the man who did mean harm toward your Alpha and who nearly killed my friend?"

Chad slapped his hands on the counter and leaned over it, shoving his face in mine. I forced myself not to step back, because then he'd know the fear I felt with him this close. "We are handling the matter. Keep your nose out of Pack business, witch. The Pack doesn't trust you. Jared will be dealt with on our terms. Do you understand?"

I shuddered, unable to stop myself.

Chad had been much friendlier before. It was almost like the wolves had sunk their claws into him after what happened. Like his Pack members had given him a lesson on why not to trust people like myself. I hadn't done this intentionally. Why was I being accused when I'd feared for my life?

"He hurt my friend. He needs to pay for what he's done." The words squeaked out.

"I'm aware." A sliver of regret passed through his eyes, but then it was gone. "However, he is, and will remain, a Pack issue. Drop it. It's better for us to deal with this, even if it takes some time—" Chad grunted and shook his head as if he'd already said too much.

"What do you mean, *takes some time*? My friend could have died. Your wolves place little value on anyone other than themselves." Tears threatened to spill from my eyes, but I held them in check. Customer or not, Chad was an asshole. I wanted, no, I *needed* him out.

"The Pack follows the traditions. If it didn't, there would be anarchy. Would you like werewolves roaming the city, chewing on unsuspecting prey? If that's what you want, little red, the wolves are already hungry for your blood. Your own wolf would be killed alongside you." With a huff, Chad took two steps away from the counter. "Besides, don't forget that the moron requested the poison from you. He wanted to kill my father, and we haven't forgotten that. His crimes go beyond nearly killing your friend."

The anger gleaming in Chad's eyes dissolved my own. His dad had almost died, and Jared had nearly gotten away with it. I couldn't be too upset with Chad.

"Why did you come here?" I bit my lower lip. The bell chimed, signifying another customer, and a tall brunette woman walked through the door. "No loitering is allowed in the store, sir," I said, unable to come up with a better line.

His shoulders shook as if he were trying to stop himself from doubling over with laughter. He leaned in close so only I could hear his next remark. "I threaten you and your boyfriend, and the best you can throw at me is loitering?"

I jerked away, seeing the error of my ways. The female customer glanced in our direction, and I smiled, trying to be reassuring. My attention zeroed back on Chad, hoping he'd get out as soon as possible. I didn't need trouble from the wolves, and I certainly didn't need it while I was dealing with Eternally Magick.

"I want to try one of your potions." He dug out a scrap of paper from his pocket. "Don't poison me."

The potion in question surprised me. What he wanted was something for nerves. I couldn't imagine why he'd come asking for this. Didn't wolves have their own way of coping with stress?

"I have some on hand," I said. "Just a moment, I'll get it."

The brunette placed a few baggies of herbs in her shopping tote as I passed by, trying my best not to limp. The energy drifting from her reminded me of what I experienced sometimes from Jessa. It took all my willpower not to do a double take at her. I couldn't show ineptitude within the witch community.

I grabbed a couple of vials of the stress potion, as well as a more powerful variant in case the normal dose didn't work. All of the ingredients in these should be safe since I'd made them myself. None of them contained anything that might hurt Chad. Definitely no wolf's bane but I wasn't sure if there was anything else out there that wasn't tied to werewolf lore that would affect him.

Werewolves were very resilient, so I guess I'd find out.

When I finished selecting the potions, I headed back to the counter where Chad was casting glances at the brunette. She watched him with a seductive pout on her ruby red lips.

I blinked at him, unable to comprehend what I was seeing. Chad had a beef with witches, yet he was giving googly eyes to one. *Whatever.* I set the vials in a bag and used the cash register to check him out. "Earth to Chad. The total is—"

He snapped his head in my direction. "You know my

name. What else did your boyfriend tell you? I'm sure he's holding back, not giving you the whole slice of the pie. Things you'd cringe over if you knew." He threw a fifty-dollar bill on the counter, then stalked toward the door with the bag in his hand. Stopping for a second, he glanced at the brunette then back to me. "You helped me. I won't forget that, but I'm the least of your problems, Mia."

I blinked at him, unable to form a meaningful response. "Your change?" I said sounding stupid even to myself as I held up the fifty.

"Keep the tip." With that, he walked out, and I doubted he meant the monetary tip. After I finished visiting with Jessa tonight, I *needed* to see Ethan, even if it meant stopping by his house. We had to talk; there was no way around it. What was he keeping from me?

Brunette stalked up to the counter, moving with the tote bag of herbs on her shoulder. "You're in over your head with them, child. If you want my advice, stay away from the wolves as much as you can."

My mouth dropped open. I couldn't believe she'd known what he was, but then again, she was more powerful than I was. However, not even Jessa had known werewolves were real.

"Believe me, I've been where you are. They aren't like us. Jessa spoke highly of you. Now that I've seen you for myself, I see your potential to be like your grandmother is very good. Rose was my mentor. Don't keep yourself secreted away when you could use our help." She pulled out the herbs she'd picked from the shelves so I could see their sales codes.

"You knew my grandmother?" The bag of thyme fell from my hand and thumped against the counter. I hadn't realized my grandmother was so prominent in the witch community. She had been powerful, and I knew she'd had friends, but this was... it was intense. "I'm scared of running into the wrong kind of people. It feels safer to remain in the shadows."

Brunette shrugged an elegant shoulder. "While that's true for some, you've succeeded in finding the wrong crowd all by yourself." She tapped the fifty-dollar bill still lying on the counter with one long red fingernail. "Consider my advice, doll. If you're not sure, talk to Jessa and ask her opinion. Tell her Selene stopped by. We're not a large group, but you'll learn more than you would if you remain locked in the shell you're hiding in."

"Okay, I will." I finished ringing up Selene's order, then watched her glide away with the grace of a cat.

"See you around, doll," she called over her shoulder before stepping outside. The door closed behind her.

While I didn't like branching out, I'd talk with Jessa. I only hoped Selene was true to her word, not someone else who was waiting in the wings to screw with my life.

However, I had bigger things to worry about, like wondering what Ethan was keeping from me...if he was. Maybe Chad was trying to drive a wedge between us. A simple conversation would straighten everything out, hopefully.

*W*ith Eternally Magick officially closed for the day, I swept the floor. An onslaught of curious teenagers had barged in minutes before closing, so I'd had to delay while they'd pointed and snickered.

Jessa would've frowned on me for throwing them out, but I had to make the poultice before visiting her in the hospital. My foot couldn't stand it any longer.

A catchy dubstep beat broke the shop's silence, and I pulled my cell phone from my pocket. Nolan's number flashed on the screen. Letting out a harsh sigh, I hit a button to accept the call. Why of all times did my brother have to choose now? The chances of me getting home before heading to the hospital were less and less possible. Hopefully this wouldn't take too long, because I really didn't want to deal with him, not after this morning's near miss.

"Hey sis," he said, sounding his normal chipper self. I wondered for a moment if Ethan and Nolan had talked further after I left, or maybe it was just that Nolan was off work. However, from the sounds of him driving and the car horns, I didn't think he was home just yet.

"Hi Nolan. What's up?" I tried to keep my tone as natural as possible. If he suspected anything, then I couldn't be the one to let that happen. If Ethan gave anything away, that was his problem, not mine. I'd do what I could to hold up our relationship's secrecy.

"Driving home. I had to drop off my girl since she's having car problems." The faint clicking of a turn signal in the background had me wondering how close he was to Ethan's place. "How are you doing?"

"I'm good. Just finishing up at my friend's store." I hated talking with him about this, but my family was nosy and they knew I was working. It was just a matter of time before they figured it out for themselves. Besides, I still might need assistance, since I'd thought I would have gotten a job weeks before now, if not months.

"Ah, it was called something like Witchy Business, wasn't it?" He chuckled. That deep rumbling sound infuriated me faster than any other noise could.

I propped the broom in the back where Jessa usually kept it. There were a few other chores, but I'd save those for the morning when I had to keep myself awake. The werewolf book went back in her office where it'd stay. If I needed any information, I'd ask someone who would know the facts, not just lore. "Nolan, that's not funny."

"Sure it is, sis." He kept going, not giving me a chance to add a defensive reply. "Anyways, I was wondering if you're missing anything."

So this is how it was going to go. He was trying to get me riled up in hopes that I'd spill my guts. No, I wouldn't fall for that. "What do you mean?" I asked.

"You know, you spent a few nights over at my place after the mugging incident. Could you have lost something?" He prodded me like he was getting more frustrated the longer we talked, but this could work out to my advantage.

"I don't follow. I'm pretty sure I have my belongings. I don't know what you're trying to get at—"

"Your purple hairbrush." He huffed. "I found it in the bathroom this morning. Do you know anything about that?"

Biting my lower lip, I scrambled for a clever comeback. Nothing came to mind.

"You still there?" he asked.

I grabbed my keys and purse. "Oh, that brush. I've been looking for it. I thought it was gone, so I bought a new one. When can I come by and pick it up?" Maybe this would be my excuse to talk with Ethan for a couple minutes while Nolan grabbed the brush. At least I could try to figure out what he was keeping from me.

"Sorry for the questions. I just... Never mind. You can swing by tonight. It's no problem."

"Thanks, Nolan." I stopped in front of the door. My ankle had started swelling pretty badly because I had been standing a lot throughout the day.

A bell chimed over the phone, signaling he was probably home by now. "Don't mention it. I know how much you hate to lose anything. This was just a misunderstanding. Forget I said anything."

He was right I did hate losing things, which made my current situation that much worse. If the truth ever came out now, I couldn't feign ignorance.

"Okay, see you later." The phone beeped, and I squeezed my hand around my keys, feeling the metal dig painfully into my palm.

Nolan hated liars, and now I'd betrayed him.

4

ETHAN

*T*he familiar rumble of an engine drew me toward the window. All the other guys typically arrived later, so it had to be Nolan. I wasn't exactly excited about tonight, but it had been a while since I'd played.

This was the second poker night of the year, and I'd missed so much during my deployment and even after I'd returned, as I'd spent lots of time with Mia and Chad because of my impending transformation.

Frankly, I'd have a harder time sitting back and connecting with the guys now, especially after the argument with Nolan. Perhaps I didn't know how to be myself anymore.

There were so many things I had to control. My hearing, sense of smell, sight and strength were vastly improved. Plus I had a more of a temper. Anger rose quicker, as if the beast held more power over me.

I did a few jumping jacks to try loosening up a little. The more physical I got, the better.

Last night's rumble in the sack with Mia came to mind, and I wiped away my grin. Our sex life was on fire. The beast connected to her as if she was our mate. My heart knew that was true, but I clung to who I thought I was. Relationships weren't part of my big picture... at least they hadn't been. Being with Mia changed all of that.

Keys jingled in the lock, and I darted into the kitchen before Nolan came in. When he was inside, I walked into the living room to greet him. "Hey, buddy, how was your day?"

Nolan nodded, holding up two six packs of beer. "Pretty good. Had to drop off my girl before hitting the store. She's not a fan of poker nights. I didn't want to raise her suspicions." He headed past me to the kitchen. "How was yours?"

With how much we drank and gambled, I could see why she wasn't crazy about the male bonding. However, I hadn't met his current girlfriend. Probably due to our rocky friendship, but I hoped to start mending that.

"It was good. Did some cleaning in preparation for tonight. Work begins again tomorrow, so I can't have too many of those." I waved at the beer. Although my appetite was a lot heartier than it had been, I'd still lost weight in the past few weeks. Would the alcohol affect me like it used to? Regardless, I wasn't about to chance it.

"The place looks nice. Thanks." Nolan glanced over his shoulder. "Looking forward to work?"

"Actually I am." He cocked an eyebrow at me like I was crazy. "Besides, my dad would've been proud of me." I leaned against the counter, the memory of my father weighed heavy on my heart. Nolan understood who I was. He'd been my best friend since we were babies.

"Yeah, he would be." He patted my shoulder. "I'll order some pizza, if you'll get the card table set up."

This was what I remembered, not these stressful last few weeks. We were going to be fine as long as he never found out about my relationship with Mia. That idea wasn't realistic, unless Mia and I went our separate ways. The beast slammed against the wall of my chest, and I clenched my hands into fists. Pain radiated through my torso and the wolf ripped at my insides, like he was trying to claw his way out of me.

Chad had said that when I felt this way, I needed to get away from others and the source of the stress. I had to focus on something else. However, the person I would normally focus on to make myself feel better happened to be a cause of my current situation.

I headed to the garage to grab the card table, taking a few deep calming breaths.

My cell phone vibrated in my pocket and I checked the caller ID and saw Chad's number. Now wasn't the time. Did he have some kind of psychic connection? No, I refused to think along those lines. That didn't fit the folklore I'd heard about werewolves, but it didn't mean it wasn't possible. After all, I was secretly dating a witch.

I ignored the call, but he tried again. This time, I just let the phone vibrate. The Pack couldn't expect me to be at their disposal whenever they felt it was time to meet. Some people needed to maintain a normal life. Besides, I wasn't even a full member yet. They'd made that painfully clear.

The phone buzzed a third time. I grabbed the table, trying to remain calm, but each ring brought me closer to losing my temper.

Finally, a few text message alerts chimed on my phone. I'd see what he had to say, then I'd turn off my phone. The messages were far from what I'd expected.

CHAD

Important meeting.

Call me back now.

A member's life is in danger. We need your help.

I nearly dropped the phone. My brain calculated my options and why they needed my help. What if they were just trying to lure me in, knowing this was the type of message I'd most likely respond to? But what I knew of Chad told me he wasn't the type to manipulate others into doing his will.

"Find the table yet?" Nolan called. His booted footsteps traveled over the carpet, heading in my direction. "I doubted you'd need help lifting it, Army man."

I shoved the phone in my pocket, walking to the door before he could poke his head into the garage and find me messing with my phone. "No, I've got it."

He stood in the doorway with raised his eyebrows. "Apparently. What were they feeding you over there?"

I looked at the table then back at him, not sure what he was getting at.

"You're holding the table like it's nothing." He jabbed a playful fist to my abs, then he shook his hand. "Ouch. You're ripped. You'll have to teach me your tricks."

The doorbell rang in the house and we headed inside.

The last thing he needed was to learn my 'tricks', since I didn't think he'd like being a werewolf any more than I did. However, I couldn't change the past; the only thing I could do was hope I could live a fairly normal life with my girl, my best friend, and the only family I had now.

I set about rearranging the furniture in the living room to make space for the card table, while Nolan answered the door. "Uh, sorry. We're not interested."

"I'm one of Ethan's friends." Chad's voice set my nerves on fire. That asshole. "If I could talk to him—"

"Since when? He didn't mention anyone dropping by.

We're busy. You should come back later." Nolan started to shut the door, but Chad held it open.

The energy pouring off Chad made my skin crawl. I jogged to the door to intervene. Chad wasn't happy, and I wasn't thrilled with him being here either. Perhaps I could peacefully send him on his way. While he had a missing Pack member, I couldn't be expected to get involved. I wasn't one of them yet.

"What are you doing here?" I said, stepping between Chad and Nolan. Nolan stayed where he was with arms crossed over his chest. He looked like he wouldn't budge. "Can I have a moment?"

Nolan sighed, throwing his hands in the air. "Just don't take too long. The guys will arrive any minute now."

I knew very well that they'd be here soon. If I had any hope of getting Chad to leave, then I needed space. "Want to go make some nachos? They're always a hit."

"The pizza is... Fine. I'll go." Nolan grumbled under his breath. If I'd wanted to, I could have caught what he was saying, but right now, I was more interested in why Chad stood on my doorstep. Or maybe even more curious about how he'd found my house in the first place. But he probably had his ways.

I stepped on the porch, closing the door behind me. "What the fuck are you doing here?" Cold air sent chills over my arms, but my frustration warmed me.

"I tried calling and texting. I was even polite to your roommate, but you should know your place. I'm your superior. The only one who gives a rat's ass about your life. You need to help me out too." Chad shook with pent-up anger, looking like he could come unhinged at any moment.

At least I wasn't alone in those feelings.

"It's serious." He locked eyes with me in challenge and I lowered my gaze. "He's a good kid, and he's been missing for a few weeks now. His brother noticed he wasn't at the last meeting, so he tried calling. The idiot didn't think to check his fucking voicemail sooner."

Chad turned away, leaning against the railing on the porch. "There's something suspicious about the voicemail message. You're in the military. Don't ask how I know. So I think you'd be a good asset in this." He glanced over his shoulder at me, this time not challenging me. "Plus, you could prove yourself to the Alpha and other high ranking members."

While I hated being sucked into this, he made several good points. I did have skills that could help, and if I did this they might accept me more readily. Perhaps I could use it as a bargaining chip for them to leave Mia and me alone.

"Fine. I'll help. What do you need me to do?" A truck pulled up to the curb, and both Chad and I looked at my friends hopping out.

"Looks like you have quite an evening planned. The Pack is meeting in two hours. You can entertain your friends a little, but you need to be at this address. Promptly." He handed me a scrap of paper, and I glanced down at it before shoving the note in my jeans.

"Okay, I'll be there. You can't show up whenever you damn well feel like it." Even though Chad had taught me about dominance issues amongst the wolves, I couldn't let this stand, not when I had a lot to lose if anyone found out I was a werewolf now.

Nolan was already suspicious, and I didn't need to add to his suspicions. However, it might throw him off a little. Maybe he wouldn't pay so close attention to Mia and me if he saw Chad around. But I didn't want him to think the worst of me, regardless of the deception.

Chad stood straighter. He was an inch or two shorter than me. However, his power more than made up for his

33

stature. "If you would have answered your damn phone, I wouldn't have had to impose." With that, he hurried down the porch steps, heading off to his dark green Jeep.

My friends looked from him to me as they walked up the sidewalk to the porch. "Everything okay?" Tony asked.

"It's fine. Just someone I know." I opened the door. Nolan sat at the card table munching on nachos looking grumpy. When he saw the other guys, he got up from his chair and put on his usual grin.

At least one of us could put on a happy façade.

5

MIA

*I*n between Ethan this morning and my ankle, I just longed to fall into bed with a healing poultice wrapped around my ankle and sleep. Instead, I was sitting at Jessa's bedside.

She looked much better than she had, but I couldn't fight the stirring guilt I got each time I came by. If I hadn't waited so long to get in touch with her, I might've noticed something was wrong. Only when I needed supplies did I know that werewolf scum had hurt her.

I took a deep breath, then did my best to smile. "How are you feeling today?"

She tightened her grip on my hand. "I'm on the mend. The doctor is pretty cute, so it's not horrible in here, but I can't wait to get out." Sighing, she leaned her head back. "Thanks for running the shop while I'm not able to."

"You don't need to thank me! You're my best friend, and..." If I let on about my feelings of guilt she'd lecture me again, and I wasn't in the mood for that. "I'm glad to help." However, with my finances running thin, I needed more money or a better job, and helping out interfered with job interviews.

"What aren't you saying?" Jessa paled a little.

"Nothing. Everything's fine." Part of me wanted to tell her the whole story: that sooner or later I wouldn't be able to keep helping her because of my own finances. Besides, I might be better off leaving if the werewolf Pack were going to be breathing down my neck. But I couldn't turn my back on her. Not yet.

"What aren't you saying, Mia? You're a terrible liar, so don't try to hold back from me. I'm here for you. Don't let this hospital bed torment you. Talk to me." She propped herself up in the bed a little, but winced and settled back.

"Everything's fine. Just… my parents aren't happy with me running the shop. My finances aren't great and I know you can't give me any more for helping. Plus, there's a problem with the werewolves. They're not thrilled with me after what happened." I leaned forward in the chair, not wanting anyone to overhear. There had been too much grief already without me adding more to Jessa's plate.

"Wait, what? You're dealing with the werewolves again? You should stay away from them, Mia. They're dangerous. You've already seen that." Concern filled her gaze and she reached out her hand for mine.

I knew she was worried, especially after what had happened to her. She'd had the worse end of the stick when dealing with Jared, but I understood what she meant. However, I couldn't say I would stay away from all werewolves. Ethan was becoming a werewolf, and I didn't want to give up my relationship with him, even if I questioned it more and more.

"I didn't go after the werewolves to talk with them. I just…" I waved my hands, trying to retreat from the conversation before she could pull me into telling her more.

"Mia, hon, what aren't you saying? You know you can talk to me about anything. I may have a strong opinion on a lot of things, but I'm here for you." Her tone changed from the mentor to the best friend.

Biting my lower lip, I weighed the pros and cons of filling her in, but I didn't want to put more stress on her.

She leveled her gaze at me in that strong-willed way of hers.

If I stayed any longer, I would spill my guts to her, and that wasn't on my calendar. I'd only wanted to check in on how she was healing. I rose to leave, heading to the door, which led to the hallway. The door slammed in my face.

I leapt back from it. My heart raced at the sudden smack of wood against the doorframe. When I looked at her, she frowned with her hand outstretched. The door hadn't closed from an odd gust of wind. She'd used her powers to keep me here, regardless of the cost to her still healing body.

Any concern I felt shifted away as the lock clicked in place. Once again, she was bullying me into giving her something, and I didn't have to stand for it. While she was my mentor, I didn't need the grief that being under her had dealt me. If it weren't for her, neither Ethan nor myself would be in the situation we were in.

"No, you're not going to do this. If you don't back down, so help me." I clenched my hands into fists. I wouldn't retaliate with magic. She wasn't my enemy and I didn't want to ruin our relationship further.

"What do you think you're going to do? You're in a hospital. If you won't practice your craft in your own home, you won't do so here." Jessa leaned back in the bed. The paleness of her skin showed that she'd strained herself with the display. I didn't want her weakening herself further when I knew how hard she'd fought to get better again.

Her words hit hard. She might've been right about that a

few weeks ago, but I was becoming a different person, a different witch. Now I knew there was real danger in the world, and I wasn't willing to charge into battle unprepared, not if it could claim the lives of the ones I loved and who loved me.

The frustration I'd felt withdrew from me. I limped back to the bedside and eased myself into the chair. "Fine. If you want to know, several things happened in the shop. I found the book on werewolves you keep in the office. I read some of it, and... I'm concerned." Even though I didn't want to go through this with her, the sooner I got it off my chest, the faster she'd get off my back. "I don't know how much of it is true and how much is just lore."

Jessa frowned but she didn't say anything.

"It's not just the Pack that concerns me, since I don't really deal with them personally." At least I hadn't until today's impromptu meeting with Chad. "I'm more worried about Ethan, as I don't want anything happening to him. It's already too late to save him from his fate, but if he becomes a monster like what I've read about..." I sighed. "How can I be in a relationship with him?"

"Maybe you shouldn't, hon." Sadness darkened Jessa's eyes. "It's not something you want to hear, but for wolves, the Pack is a stronger tie than anything else. Don't expect his complete loyalty to be yours once he becomes one of them."

I hated hearing that because after what I'd read I knew it was true. Besides, I still didn't know what to make of my encounter with Chad today. He'd been more aggressive than before.

"What happened with your foot?" Jessa prodded. I looked up at her, and she stared at me with a look of utmost patience.

"It's a long story." She didn't want me to be with Ethan. If I told her he was the reason this happened, it would be one more piece of evidence that proved she was right. "One I'm not sure I want to go into at the moment."

"Give me the short version?" Her lips quirked as mischief chased across her features. "Sounds like an interesting tale, and I've been watching too much Jerry Springer to pass up on this."

"Let's just say I jumped out of a second floor window. End of story." That already felt like too much information. She'd probably just ask more questions. However, I was surprised that she sat there silently with wide eyes. "You're not going to push me into telling you more?"

She placed her index finger and her thumb by the corner of her mouth and pretended to zip her lips closed, then she shook her head. Maybe she was right. I'd put myself, my relationship with my brother and family and more all at risk because of Ethan, yet I didn't want to separate from him.

We quietly watched each other, and I expected her to pop at any minute with the questions brewing inside her. My thoughts went back to the shop, Chad and the brunette. I wouldn't tell Jessa about Chad, but Selene was something I could mention before I left.

"There was something else I needed to talk to you about." I ran a hand through my hair. "A woman came in today named Selene. She told me to ask you about her. She said she knew my grandmother."

Jessa blinked at me, keeping her face carefully neutral. "Selene? Are you sure?" She shook her head. "I know her."

That wasn't exactly the response I'd been expecting. Most of the time when Jessa talked about magic and other witches, she was more enthusiastic and perky. Granted, I'd forgive her lack of perkiness due to being in the hospital, but I was surprised to find her taken aback. "What's wrong?"

"Nothing. It's been a while since I've talked with her.

What did she want?" She sat up a little in the hospital bed as if this was something she needed to give her full attention.

"She knows I need to build up my skills and that I've fallen in with the wrong people... er...werewolves. She said she can help, and that I shouldn't hide myself from others who could give me assistance." I scratched the back of my neck, no longer thinking that bringing up Selene had been such a good idea.

"I know what she's trying to do. She's luring you away from me. Her group helped me get to where I am with my powers, but I spoke to your grandmother. I know what she wanted for you. They would make you into one of them and harness your powers." Tightness creased the corners of her eyes and lips giving her a haunted look.

"What do you mean? How could they do something like that? Harness my powers?" I had never heard of such a thing. I'd always thought power and magic were individual abilities. Some witches joined together, but they were still single beings. Just the magic was brought together to greater impact a situation. One person didn't use the others for their own purposes.

"Just what I said. Don't trust her, hon. If she comes by the shop again, I want you to call me." Jessa sounded deadly serious. But what could she do? She was in the hospital. She wouldn't climb out of her bed and come 'rescue' me. Or would she?

"I'll call." I glanced at the clock. Visiting hours were ending soon and I needed to get out before the nurse shooed me away.

"When you get home, make a poultice for that foot and keep it elevated. You're just making it worse. If it doesn't heal, you could have to see a doctor." She rolled her eyes and looked around the room. "Don't forget to add some comfrey to it and rest—"

"Yes, mother. It's not my first time dealing with something like this." Maybe not of this severity, but I'd twisted my ankle before. Seeing Jessa concerned about me was sweet, though, especially considering she was in a far worse condition than I was. "Get some rest, and I'll come pester you in a day or so."

She smiled. "I look forward to hearing the longer version of that story."

Grimacing, I knew she did, but I didn't know if I wanted to tell. Maybe it'd be something funny to look back on eventually. However, Nolan could never know, and if I told Jessa...

I shook the thoughts away and waved goodbye.

6

ETHAN

*T*he clock ticked as the minutes went by, and no matter what I tried, I couldn't get comfortable, even with the amount of alcohol I'd consumed. This whole evening was awkward. Partly I wasn't quite used to spending time together with everyone. From the look on Nolan's face, he wanted to talk about what was going on, but that wasn't the best idea.

"This hand will be for the last slice of pizza. Who's in?" Tony sloppily shuffled the cards, then dealt them out to everyone.

Unfortunately for me, I was running out of time, and the party didn't seem to be stopping anytime soon. I knew from past experience these things sometimes lasted until the wee hours. How was I going to get out of this without offending anyone?

Telling them I was going to bed and trying to sneak out through a window wouldn't work. I needed my car to get to the location. When I'd been overseas, I'd thought about being back home, wanting to be close to those I loved again. Now I sometimes wished I was back over there. At least life had been simpler. I'd been a normal man, not in the process of becoming a werewolf.

"Fold." I set down my cards, not really feeling the game anymore.

Tony cocked an eyebrow at me, but he shrugged and returned his drunken attention to the game. Jim was drunker than Tony, and I was pretty sure they'd have to spend the night here, what with the amount of alcohol they'd drunk. However, Nolan had imbibed the least. He sipped on his beers slower, keeping his mind clearer.

The doorbell rang and my hackles went up. Who was it now? If Chad was back, then so help me... However, I couldn't figure out any reason for him to be here. He'd given me the information I needed to meet the Pack, and I still had time before I had to be there. Although, I did need to start wrapping things up soon. I just had to figure out how I'd do that.

Nolan rose to get the door, but I waved him back to the game. "It's okay. I'll get it."

"All right." He kept his gaze on me, watching my every move.

I headed off to the door, tired of him doing that. When I opened the door, I nearly slammed it again. What in the hell was Mia doing here? She hadn't told me she'd be stopping by. She said she would be with her friend until late.

"What are you—" I cleared my throat, knowing Nolan wasn't far away. The last thing I needed to do was act even more uncomfortable. "Hi Mia. We're playing poker. Nolan's right over there."

She frowned at me. From the look in her eye, there was something bothering her. "Thanks. Nolan called. I'm here to pick up my brush. He said he found it around here."

I stepped aside to let her in and wondered exactly how much Nolan had said. I just hoped he hadn't tried to press her too hard; if his behavior toward me was anything to go by, then I wondered if she might've been subject to it as well.

Nolan rose from his chair and grabbed a plastic grocery bag from the coffee table. "Here you go, sis."

"Thanks. I guess I'm off now." She looked between us as if waiting for something. "Have fun with poker night." However, she didn't walk back out the door.

"Do you want a beer or something?" Nolan asked, his eyebrows drawing together.

She sucked in a breath. "Oh no, sorry. Night, guys." She waved to Tony and Jim, then strode away casting a glance over her shoulder.

When Nolan shut the door, I grimaced. Now I needed to make my escape. If I didn't go soon, I might be late, and that was the last thing I needed.

"Sorry guys. I have to go to the store, gas up my car, and get a few things, since I start work tomorrow." Worst excuse ever, but I didn't know what else to say.

"Aww, man. Really? That's lame." Jim set down his cards and stretched back in the chair. "Why didn't you get it done earlier?"

Good question. "Guess I wanted to savor my last free day. It slipped my mind." I waved. "Be back a bit later." I nodded to Nolan. "Night."

"Good night." He lowered his voice so only the two of us could hear. "When you get back, we're talking."

I forced a smile. "Sure thing." Then I shoved my feet into my shoes, tucked the laces inside them, and walked out.

---

*W*hen I'd gotten a little distance from the house, I called Mia. I didn't have a lot of time to talk, but I wanted to see what her visit had been about. Her phone rang and rang before she finally answered.

"Sorry," I said. "Were you sleeping?"

"No, I was busy working on... never mind. It's nothing. I need to talk to you." The softest wisp of anger filled her voice, and I wondered what was going on.

This wasn't like her. Something had to have happened. What had Nolan said?

"What's up? Everything okay?" Then again, I had every right to feel upset. She'd jumped out of the fucking window instead of waiting for her brother to leave. The siblings were trying to drive me crazy. "How's your ankle?" I asked, letting a little of my own anger slip free.

She sputtered and groaned. "Wait, I can explain. But first, you should tell me what Chad meant when he said there are things you're keeping from me."

Damn. Chad had something else coming to him. If he wanted my help, then he needed to promise he'd shut his mouth when it came to Mia. The fact he'd seen her made my blood pressure soar. The Pack didn't like her at all, so I couldn't help the fear that someone might hurt her out of revenge for what she'd almost done to their Alpha. "I don't know what you're talking about. I told you this morning what was going on."

"Somehow I don't know if I believe that. I really want to, but it's hard since it took this morning for me to know the Pack had thought of killing you. It's possible you're keeping other things from me." She sighed, sounding wary. "I want you to feel comfortable talking to me. I've told you so much about myself. I just don't want to feel like you're pushing me away from your other self."

If I could have slammed my fist against the steering wheel without second-guessing the force I'd use would break it, I would've. This was the worst time for her to be getting into this kind of discussion with me. I appreciated the fact she wanted to know what was going on. However, this werewolf situation was new to me, and I was having a hard enough time trying to take care of her and myself, without our new relationship get stomped down by all the opposition.

"Mia, babe, this isn't a good time." Especially since I was getting closer to the location where the werewolves met, which not surprisingly was out on the outskirts of town surrounded by lush woods.

"Why? I'm trying to open up. It's hard enough to pretend in front of Nolan without things getting too awkward. But when it's just you and me, I want to feel like you care enough to talk to me."

The whistling of a teakettle shrilled, nearly making me drop the phone. My ears were too good at picking up sound and loud noises were still something I was struggling with. I didn't want my hearing obliterated.

"I have to go to a Pack meeting. That's why. I promise I'll give you a call later if you're still awake. Promise." However, I had no idea how long this thing would last. "I've got to go now, babe. I'll talk to you later."

"Talk to you later. Love you." She sounded so sad when she said those words that it ripped at my heart.

"I love you too." Just as I put my phone away, there was a knock at my window. I nearly jumped out of my seat, but it was just Chad. I hadn't heard him approach, but then again, the wolves were a lot stealthier than I was.

Chad opened my car door then stepped out of reach. "You were talking to your girl, huh? Make sure the phone is off. Disruptions during the meeting are punishable."

He'd told me this before, so I fished my phone out again and turned it off. I didn't know what punishment for his people meant, but being in the military, I didn't have any rose-colored delusions.

"It's off." I looked up at him and slid the phone in my jeans pocket. "Let's get this done."

Chad slapped me on the back. "That's the attitude. You're already starting to fit in. I can only imagine how you'll be when you're an actual wolf."

That's exactly what I was afraid of.

We walked into the majestic mansion. I'd never been in someplace like this before. Men and a few women lingered in the corridor, watching me...sizing me up. They were dressed in all manners of clothes from jeans and t-shirts to suits.

Thankfully, Chad was dressed in a pair of faded jeans and a snarky t-shirt, so I didn't feel underdressed. "Now that we're all here, let's head into the meeting hall," he called out, raising his voice over the low hum of conversation.

Regardless of the fact I'd been early, I was still the last one to arrive. This was off to a great start. I had no idea what Chad or any of these werewolves expected from me.

When we headed into the hall, there were seats set up like an auditorium. I grabbed a spot in the back, while Chad strode up front and took a seat in one of the chairs facing the audience beside another younger man about our age—that was, if werewolves aged at the same rate as humans. However, from what I'd learned so far, I wasn't exactly sure that was true.

Once everyone was settled in their seats, a gentleman I recognized as the Alpha stood in front of the group. He didn't need a microphone. For one thing, werewolves had sensitive enough hearing, so unless he was whispering very, very softly, everyone in the room would hear him. Plus, he had a booming authoritative voice that reminded me of a drill sergeant I knew.

For the first time in a while, I didn't feel quite as awkward around these people. I could relate to the hierarchy and an authoritative leader. The supernatural was the only element that made me uncomfortable.

"Good evening. Most of you should know why I've called everyone out here on such short notice." The Alpha glanced back at the young male sitting next to Chad, both of whom lowered their gazes. "One of our young members named Jacob Armstrong is missing. I strongly suspect there's something amiss. Jacob is not one to run. Plus he left a voicemail for his brother, Shane," the Alpha said, waving a hand at the guy next to Chad, "which proves our reason for concern. Not only is his life in jeopardy, but I think there's something else going on here. The whole Pack and our race could be in danger."

Chad handed his father a digital recorder, then returned to his seat.

I couldn't believe that when I was close to becoming a werewolf, the Pack was having problems of this magnitude. My concerns about my career and my relationship with Mia seemed less worrisome and intense.

"Shane, I need your help," a young man's deep voice came through the recorder. "They're after us. These men... they're studying us—" A soft thud made me think he'd dropped his phone. "Shit!" Tires squealed and an engine revved, as another set of tires screeched. There was someone after him, but what did he mean about people studying them?

The loud crunch of metal as two cars impacted nearly had me reaching to plug my ears, but I kept my hands fisted in my lap.

"Damn it! It'll be okay, baby. I'll get us out of this. We still have hope." A low murmuring stared in the room, but the Alpha cut it off with a wave of his hand. There was the sound of a car door being squeaked open, and a couple of tranquilizer guns firing off a few darts.

"Let's get them back to the facility." This guy sounded like a mercenary, or maybe a high-dollar security guard. "The doctor is pissed that two of his best specimens are on the loose. If they had escaped, I'm not sure we would still have jobs."

"I don't know what to think about what we're doing. Look at them. They're kids. I don't see what's so wrong with them that they'd have to be locked in a place like this." His partner had a conscience, and he questioned the cause, which meant he hadn't been there for long. Maybe he'd give enough information to figure out where they were.

"Don't talk that way. I'd hate to have to report your behavior. You have plenty of potential. Now do something with the car. Maybe drive it into the woods and burn it."

"Ugh," the softer of the two men said, then the recording cut off.

I leaned back in the chair, wishing I had more background on all involved. Jacob had said 'us', which meant there was someone with him. Still, I couldn't figure out why these werewolves wanted me to help them.

"Your brother is apparently with a woman at this research facility. Has he said anything about having any relationships?" the Alpha asked.

Shane's gaze shifted between Chad and his leader, looking as if the Pope had just spoken to him. "No, sir, he didn't. He spent full moons with Alayna on occasion, but that's all I know about his love life."

The Alpha looked into the crowd of people, and several people sitting around a certain tall, blond female stared straight at her. "Alayna?"

She shook her head. "Alpha, I don't know anything about Jacob having relationships outside of ours. He doesn't seem exactly thrilled to stick around or come by unless there's a full moon, but he didn't call me last month. I figured he was with someone else in the Pack."

The Alpha turned his attention back to Shane. "Do you know who he was with at the full moon? I'm assuming that's the last time anyone saw him. That was a couple nights before the voicemail, wasn't it?"

Shane cleared his throat and squirmed a little under the Alpha's scrutiny. "That was exam week, so he was off studying with one of his college friends. I didn't really ask for details. I figured he'd come by later, but when he didn't, I just assumed he was busy, sir."

"You didn't think to get in touch with him?" The Alpha crossed his arms over his impressive chest.

"We're brothers, but that doesn't mean we're joined at the hip." Chad subtly elbowed Shane in the side, making Shane wince and cough a little. "Sir," he added.

"You're his older brother. It's your responsibility to look out for him. If anything happens to Jacob, you'll pay for it dearly." The Alpha nodded to Chad, who grabbed the other man by the upper arm.

The fact Shane hadn't gotten in touch with his brother, or seemingly even tried to, boggled my mind. It reinforced the fact that my relationship with Nolan needed to be patched up, and soon. While we weren't blood, I couldn't even imagine something like this happening between us. We looked out for one another as if we were related. Shane had a brother that was blood, yet he hadn't. My anger increased on Jacob's behalf.

Quiet chatter arose from the crowd again. The Alpha looked back at the audience. Once again, the talking simmered down. His gaze scanned faces and he jerked his head in my direction. I sat up straighter, feeling the full force of his gaze like a physical weight.

"As some of you might know, we have a new person with us. Ethan Parker will be joining the Pack when the next full moon rises. My former second in command bit him without my permission, but my son convinced me to look beyond Jared's insubordination and give Ethan a chance." He waved a hand to me. I wasn't sure if he wanted me to stand or if he was just trying to make me feel more uncomfortable, so I stood straight, keeping my hands at my sides.

The Alpha nodded, looking impressed.

All eyes in the room landed on me. I kept my attention toward the front, not wanting to see the expressions on their faces. It was better if I just focused on the Alpha. Right now, he was my biggest obstacle and the one who would determine my fate. I would follow what Chad said, and hopefully, all would be okay.

However, I couldn't help but see a few of the girls in the group, especially Alayna, casting smug glances my way. What did they know that I didn't? While they were pretty, I only had eyes for Mia. There was no other girl for me.

"That will be all. I'll update everyone with more information when I'm able to. For now, if you notice anything suspicious about your fellow wolves, let me know." The Alpha turned away from the audience and I started for the door. Since the meeting was over, I could finally have that conversation with Mia. "I'll speak with you in private, Ethan."

The hair on the back of my neck rose, and I froze at the commanding voice requesting my presence. Other wolves walked by me, watching me with fascination. That set me on edge even more.

"Welcome," Alayna said as she slunk by, running a hand over my arm. "Maybe I'll see you around."

Something about her smile drew me in, but that's what

she was going for. She had that seductive edge to her, and I could see why Jacob had spent some of his full moons with her. However, I could also see how a smart guy would see past her façade.

I refused to fall for her whims. I had my own girl waiting for me.

7

MIA

*T*he cell phone played its upbeat, catchy ringtone, and I stretched my arms and legs, immediately regretting the last part. My aching foot was propped up on the arm of the couch. I shut off the television, unable to believe I'd fallen asleep while waiting for Ethan. How long had it been since he'd called the first time?

"Hello?" My voice rasped a little, and I cleared my throat trying not to sound as sleepy as I felt.

"Hey, babe." If I was tired, then Ethan sounded exhausted. "Sorry, I should've texted first to see if you were awake. I can call back in the morning. It'd have to be pretty early since I'm working tomorrow, or I won't be in touch until afterwards. It'll be a long day."

"What happened at the meeting? Is everything okay?" From the way he sounded, I guessed it wasn't. However, I wanted to hear it from him. Besides, I wondered what exactly the Pack meeting had been about, especially if they had Ethan there. Was it just a welcoming meeting? Then again, that didn't make sense, because wouldn't that have been planned? Could it be about Jared?

"It's fine. They just wanted to talk with me about what's going on with one of their members. That's all." He gave a sleepy chuckle. "No need to worry."

I opened my mouth to dispute that last comment, cite all the things I should be worrying about, namely justice for Jessa and for him. But he was right; if I broke out into all of that now, there wouldn't be any resolution. All I would do is stress the both of us. That wouldn't help anything.

However, he was blocking our lines of communication again, bringing me right back to my previous concerns. Did I need to worry about what he was hiding from me? Could Jessa be right that I needed to just back away from Ethan?

"Babe? You're kind of quiet." Apprehension spread through Ethan's voice, and I immediately regretted my long silence.

"I'm okay. Guess I'm just tired." Normally, this would be the part of the conversation where I'd ask if he'd be coming over tomorrow, but I didn't know if that was such a good idea. My heart demanded I say something, but my head told me to give him distance.

When he was ready to talk, he'd talk. Until then, I was better off focusing on my magic, taking care of Jessa's shop, and keeping a low profile with Nolan, especially after how things had been earlier at the poker night. Things had seemed too tense as it was, without me further agitating the situation. I wished I hadn't even gone over to get the stupid brush.

"Right. I'll let you get back to sleep. Good night. Love you."

"Love you too. Good night, Ethan." I set the phone down, but part of me felt so hollow. The bulletproof connection we shared seemed broken and I wasn't sure how to fix it.

Pain shot through my leg as I readjusted my position. If I had someone to talk to maybe I'd feel better. Jessa was in the hospital, I wasn't comfortable talking to Ethan and Nolan couldn't know about any of this, especially the supernatural part. Although the part about me and Ethan sneaking behind his back and having a relationship wasn't good to mention to him, either.

I still had Chad's number from when he'd left me the nasty note on my door, but he wasn't exactly the person I most wanted to reach out to. Perhaps when I gave Ethan enough time, he'd realize what was important and open up a line of dialogue with me.

Until then, I had to go on, business as usual.

8

ETHAN

*T*he first day back after the holiday break had gone by slowly and was tiring. The checkpoint security had doubled, and it took a while to be cleared to enter the base. Inside there was tension in the air. Something was going on. The anxiety coming from both officers and enlisted was like pins and needles to my sensitive nerves.

The wolf in me didn't like this kind of commotion. Maybe the fact that I'd been up until the wee hours didn't help either. Things were different from when I'd last been on base. Now my superiors spoke in lowered voices behind closed doors.

Here and there, I had seen signs of a third party presence. Small changes in where certain vehicles were parked, equipment placement, and backpacks left where any drill sergeant would have thrown a fit and lectured on safety regulations.

The changes made a clear statement. Whoever was here didn't need to follow our rules. A growl built in my throat, nearly slipping from my lips. I managed to get into the barracks and say hi to some of the familiar faces before the routine kicked in.

One moment everyone was relaxed from leave, the next we were a unit. It was more than changing into the uniform, more than a job; it was becoming part of something greater than us.

Being around this many people, I had a hard time concentrating. New scents that didn't belong to the barracks still lingered in the air: tobacco, alcohol and a female's perfume.

My tasks took me near the officers' area, mostly running over documentation and rosters my lieutenant was too busy to take himself. The task was monotonous, but it confirmed my suspicions. Something was going on. Everyone seemed on edge. However, I'd heard a name thrown around a couple times: Dr. Zeaman.

I might be fishing for answers to the werewolves' problem, but perhaps this could be a clue. It would solve some of my problems to wrap it all up and find the missing wolf, but I doubted things would work out this easily for me.

That wasn't the only thing upsetting me. I couldn't help but feel like my relationship with Mia was tanking. She wanted to talk, but I didn't want to hurt her.

It had been stupid to call her in the first place. But I'd wanted to hear her voice so badly, especially after the aggravating news. Not only did the Pack want me to don a cape and save the day, but regardless of what Chad had told me, no—promised—the Alpha had pulled me aside to tell me I would be hooking up with a female werewolf.

I couldn't tell Mia. She wouldn't take well to that news, and I didn't want to break her heart. Besides, I was determined to find a way out of this mess.

After work, I sat in my car outside of Mia's house. She

was home, but I wasn't exactly sure how I'd hold up under the scrutiny of her asking more questions. Besides, she'd been quiet last night, and while I believed she was tired, I also got the feeling the problem went deeper.

Pulling away from the curb, I headed home. I needed a nap before I figured out how to mend all that was either broken or on the verge of breaking, then I'd talk with Chad and hold his ass accountable for some of the shit going on. He needed to help me out here.

When I pulled into the driveway, Nolan was sitting on the porch with a beer in hand and another sitting beside him. He held the second beer up to signal he was waiting for me. Forget the nap, it looked like I'd be mending my friendship with Nolan first.

I got out of the car and headed up the sidewalk slowly, not exactly sure what to expect. He handed me the beer, and I sat beside him on the steps. "Thanks. Sorry I had to bail on poker night so early."

"I waited up for you after everyone else left. Where were you?" Nolan didn't sound angry. He spoke just like we were having a normal conversation between friends. I didn't know what made me more nervous, this or if he'd shown anger.

I hated lying, but I couldn't tell him I'd been meeting a bunch of werewolves. "It ended up taking a lot more time than I'd anticipated." I took a swig of beer, doing anything to keep from having to talk further.

"Don't bullshit me, dude. I know you're not being honest. I've known you forever. Did you spend the night at my sister's?" He didn't look at me, but he radiated with held back emotions.

I hadn't realized how it might look for me leaving so soon after Mia. *Damn it.* "No, I didn't. What I did had nothing to do with her." I stared into my beer can, wishing it would tell me some magic answer to make all of this stop. I wanted my life back to how it was before this disaster had rained on my head. If Nolan had picked me up from the airport instead of Mia, none of this would have happened. However, I wouldn't have been there to help Mia fight the werewolf.

"What did it have to do with then? We're having major trust issues. I try to not think about them, but they are there." Nolan sighed, setting down his beer.

I couldn't talk with him about being a werewolf. Mia fought so hard to keep her life normal, and she was just a witch. Albeit one with actual magical powers, but the fact I would soon be sprouting fur and claws once a month outdid her. She could keep her witchiness under wraps a lot easier than I'd be able to keep my abilities secret.

"There are things I can't really talk about," I said, opting for truth. I wiped a hand over my face, feeling the weight of the revelation. Mia was upset I wouldn't talk with her, but I just couldn't. It wasn't personal toward either sibling.

Nolan rested a hand on my shoulder. "Is it about your deployment? If you need to talk to someone about what happened over there, you know I'm here for you. Don't shut me out." He stood. "Want another beer? I'm thinking about cooking steaks."

"Sure." My mind spun. While I'd witnessed a lot overseas that I still had trouble dealing with, I hadn't intended for Nolan to think this was about my deployment. I didn't want his pity over the fact I'd served my country.

I opened my mouth to protest against his assumption, but stopped myself. "Another beer would be great." I looked up at him, meeting his gaze. "I'll try to open up. Promise."

*D*inner with Nolan had been good. We'd talked about what had happened during my deployment, even if I wanted to keep some of that bottled inside. I wasn't exactly comfortable communicating the hard moments, but this was Nolan. I trusted him like a brother, and I needed to revive his trust in me.

If there was one thing I learned last night, it was I didn't want our relationship to resemble what I'd witnessed between Shane and Jacob, the missing werewolf. I put my empty can of beer on the coffee table and watched the sports commentary on television.

Nolan was cleaning up in the kitchen when his cell phone rang. I tried to tune it out. Listening in on phone conversations was useful, but it made me feel like an intruder on others' lives. I wouldn't want someone doing it to me.

However, a female voice on the other end purred a greeting, and I couldn't help being a little curious. "Hey, sexy, are you doing anything right now?"

"Hi hon. I'm hanging out with Ethan. What's going on?"

She laughed a throaty, erotic laugh. "I could really use some company. I bought a pair of furry handcuffs I'd like to try out."

Heat flooded my cheeks, and I turned up television a few notches. While I could guess what would happen with those handcuffs, I did not need any more information, certainly not about Nolan's sex life.

No matter how hard I tried, I had a hard time focusing on the TV. However, I relaxed when Nolan walked into the living room.

"I've got to take off for a bit. I'll be home later or possibly in the morning. My girl wants to..." He struggled for words. "Uh, she wants to watch some movies. So we're going to hang out, if that's okay? I don't mean to bail on you."

"It's fine." I winked. "Have fun. Don't let her talk you into watching any chick flicks." The fact he'd be gone relieved me. If things weren't awkward between Mia and me, I'd have called her up, but they were. So I'd reach out to Chad about the female werewolf situation.

With a sigh, I reached for my cell. I dialed the number Chad had given me, partially expecting him to ignore my call. My thoughts were interrupted by a grating sound coming from the phone. The line was horrible.

"Yes?" Chad's voice came through, and the interference slowly dissipated.

"Hey, I know it's late, but we need to talk. You got a moment?" I said, tension straining my voice. "It's about last night. Your father is forcing me into a relationship with a female werewolf. I can't leave Mia for someone else."

"Politics inside the Pack right now are delicate. Trust me, you don't want to test the waters. Mia isn't in good standing with us because of what happened. If you go against what the Alpha says and complain about his decisions, he won't be as willing to ensure your safety in the end. I'm risking my name and reputation with my father to keep you alive." Chad sounded tired. "I don't think I'll be able to help."

"What do you mean? There must be something you can do. Am I expected to leave that part of my life behind for someone I barely know?" I snarled the words. I didn't care how I came across. Mia was mine, and I would not have it any other way.

"No one expects you to get busy with producing cubs, idiot. You have been given a strong nudge to court a female wolf. To woo her. We don't force mates who would kill one another." He groaned as if he was explaining all of this to a child.

Sure, they were saying this now. "How long would I have before the Alpha expects me to find someone? Can't this be postponed?" I asked. Better to know the terms fully. Maybe I could find a way out of this.

"Listen, it's late." His tone hinted at resignation. "I'll see what I can do."

"Thank you." But the connection had already been severed.

9

MIA

*M*y swollen ankle was propped on the coffee table, resting comfortably on a folded towel. The television played one of those housewife shows I'd never admit to watching.

My foot hurt more than it had before. If I hadn't been Jessa's only assistant, I wouldn't have gone in to the shop today. Being on my feet had hindered the comfrey poultice from doing its 'magic', no pun intended.

There hadn't been any crazy visitors to the shop today, which I was glad about. Part of me had wondered if Selene would be back.

However, the one thing I worried about above all was the approaching full moon. Ethan was speaking to me less, and I had a feeling he was hiding something. My suspicions were confirmed by the fact he'd been less than forthcoming about the sudden Pack meeting.

Another reason why I'd wondered about Selene was that the full moon was a time when witches performed certain rituals. I mostly knew about that through the grimoire my grandmother left behind. I had never taken part in something like that, even though Jessa tried talking me into it a few times. That was beyond my comfort zone.

My cell phone chimed its dubstep tune. The number looked familiar.

"Hey, hon," Jessa said, her voice cheery like the sun parting grey clouds. "Are you busy?"

"No, not at all." Aside from catching up on television, but that could be put off. "How are you doing? I'm surprised to hear from you. I was going to leave for the hospital in an hour or so."

"About that. I'm doing well enough that I talked the doctor into letting me go home." I was relieved to hear that. Life was slowly returning to normal. "If you could pick me up I'd really appreciate it."

The idea of driving to the hospital with my foot this sore sent me spiraling into a mild panic. Just getting home had been excruciating, so I had no idea how I'd get there and back again.

Nolan! He could take me to pick Jessa up. He'd only met her once or twice, but he was my brother. He hadn't paid me back yet for me picking up Ethan from the airport. This would be the perfect time to cash that in.

"I don't know if I can drive with my foot in the condition it's in, but—"

"Don't worry about it then. I can take a taxi." The glow to her voice faded.

"I'll see if Nolan will take me and give you a call back." I dialed Nolan's number, hoping my brother would finally be of assistance to me. After last night, I was nervous talking to him. If I'd been feeling better, I would've just driven myself without hoping he'd be there for me, though it wasn't like he always left me hanging, but I hated feeling like I had to rely on someone else.

He answered on the third ring, right when I was

considering hanging up. "Hey, sis." His voice sounded genuinely pleased, and I wondered if this was the same guy I'd talked with the other day. He'd been upset and rightly so, if I had to be honest. "How's it going?"

"Hi, I'm doing well. Just wondered if you could possibly do me a favor." I took a deep breath, trying not to feel like I was being a total burden to him. Family relied on one another when they needed help. It was within my right to ask.

"Hmm. What's the favor? I'm headed to my girlfriend's place." The happy, laid back Nolan eroded around the edges.

My mouth fell open, and I closed it, biting my lip. Okay, well... he had a life. I couldn't be upset with him. I'd just hoped the one time I needed him, he'd be there, but I wasn't entirely out of options. "It's okay. Sorry to bother you."

"Sis, I can do it later. Just let me know what's up." His tone deepened, becoming gruffer, and I wished I'd called Ethan. Unless he was busy too, then it looked like I'd be driving, even though I really, really didn't feel up to it. Taking a taxi would be more expensive than my Ramen noodle budget could afford.

"I have to pick up my friend from the hospital, but I hurt my foot earlier. I'm not up to driving, but I guess I have to do it." Sighing, I leaned my head against the back of the couch.

"Ah, sorry, I wish I could help. Do you know of anyone else? I'm sure I could call one of my buddies. Ethan was just lounging at home when I left." The dinging of Nolan's car in the background told me he was at his destination.

"Okay, I guess I'll see if I can find someone else." Having Ethan take me was a last resort option, but it would have to do. Some of Nolan's other friends were pretty derpy. I didn't like hanging out with them. They could get too 'hands on' and flirty at times, which wasn't what Jessa or I needed after all we'd been through.

"Call me if you can't find someone." A seductive female voice in the background made me realize what Nolan was probably over at his girlfriend's house for. He was getting some. That's why he couldn't take me to the hospital.

"I will."

The two of us were drifting further and further apart. I just had to let it go. He was in his own world when it came to family, and my family loved him just the way he was.

I also didn't dare ask my parents for a ride, since they and Jessa would rub on another like sandpaper, with me in the middle. Plus mom would ask about my leg and I didn't want to go there.

I called Ethan since I didn't have anyone else to ask.

Greg, my ex, would've been one of my choices when we were still together, but he was out of my life. He'd called a few times since we broke up, but I'd ignored his calls. I wasn't about to talk to him after what happened on Christmas Eve.

"Hello?" Ethan's voice touched me in places I hadn't known existed.

"Hi." I steeled myself, trying to get the words out, even though it was less about him and more about my issues with him shutting down on me. Our communication problems weren't anything new, but I still had bouts where I had trouble talking with him.

"Is everything okay?" he asked, gentleness laced with suspicion.

I tripped over the words then shut my mouth, forcing myself to take control. "I'm fine. Kind of. I just needed a favor if you're available."

"Kind of? That's not very convincing, babe. What's going on?" His voice deepened. I shuddered, enjoying the sound. However, Jessa had told me to break up with him, and now I was asking him to drive me to take her home from the hospital.

That would go over great. Not.

"I need to pick Jessa up from the hospital." Letting out a breath, I continued, "My foot isn't doing so well, so I kind of need help getting there. I'd prefer not to drive. I was wondering if perhaps you could take me."

"That's no problem. You shouldn't hesitate to ask me something like that. I'm here for you. You do realize that, don't you? Just take it easy. I shouldn't be more than five minutes."

Relief swelled in my chest. "Thank you. I really appreciate it."

"Any time, babe." He paused for a moment. Only his soft breathing filled the phone line. "I love you, Mia. You know that. I'm just dealing with things right now that are beyond the scope of my comfort levels. We both are. Just know I'm here for you whenever you need me."

My heart skipped a beat and I questioned why I had been so hard on him. Saying this made me feel much better. No matter what faced us, we'd handle it. That was what mattered, not all the uncertainties.

"I love you as well, Ethan. You have no idea how much this means to me." However, I still had to explain to Jessa why I was bringing Ethan, who she said I shouldn't be with. Then again, sometimes a girl had to go with what she knew was right for her, regardless of all that could go wrong.

Fear had eaten at my life enough, and I refused to give it any more power over me. I was stronger than that. If I'd wanted to cower under Greg, then I wouldn't have become more of my own woman and spread my wings, even when I thought I'd simply plunge out of the sky to my death.

"I'll be there soon."

"Bye." I disconnected from the call, unable to help my silly smile. Being with Ethan was everything I'd hoped for and so much more.

Dialing back Jessa, I cleared my throat, trying to get rid of the stupidly happy sound to my voice.

"Mia? Did you find someone to pick me up?" Jessa sounded worried, and I felt bad for her. She'd been in the hospital for the past few weeks. I'm sure all she wanted was to go home to her own bed and rest.

"Yes, we'll be there soon. It should be like thirty minutes max." I couldn't help but smile knowing I'd see Ethan. Our relationship had hit a slump, but I didn't feel that way now. I felt optimism and hope.

We'd get past whatever was going on because we wanted one another. Ethan said he was here for me. He wouldn't be tired of me in a few weeks or a few years. He wanted me to be his.

I felt the exact same way.

"Something tells me your brother isn't picking us up." Disappointment soured Jessa's tone. I knew she had a crush on Nolan, but I also knew it was better if she didn't get her hopes set on him. He wasn't a good choice for her. These days he changed girlfriends like some guys changed socks. Pretty frequently. He hadn't found the right one yet. At least I hoped that was simply the case.

"No, he's not."

She sighed. There was a pause before she said, "I'll see you soon."

Squeezing my eyes shut, I wished I'd just gone to bed. It always happened like this. I tried to help someone out, only to get dragged down because they wanted something else for me.

One of these days, I'd forge my own way.

10

MIA

*E*than and I sat in the car on the way to the hospital, and I glanced over at him. He had on a black shirt and a pair of jeans. The shirt was tight enough to leave little to the imagination about his chiseled chest. I loved it, but I hated that other women could so easily see his muscular body. But I knew he was my man for as long as I wanted him.

"How was your day?" he asked. His gaze slid over me, pausing to check out my breasts. That sizzling look in his eyes melted my insides, and I wished we were back at my place instead of on the way to pick Jessa up from the hospital.

Maybe we could go back when we were done to talk and get past this communication problem we had. I wanted to clear the air and go back to the way things were.

"It was fine. Pretty boring. I didn't have a lot of customers." I smiled, refusing to mention the witch I'd encountered the other day. I still wondered why she was interested in me.

"Good. How's your foot?" He returned his gaze to the

road as the light turned green. "It looks swollen. You shouldn't be going to the shop with it like that." He frowned.

"I'm okay." He'd done first aid training, so he could probably call me on my bullshit. But I didn't want him to worry. The comfrey hadn't had a chance to take care of the problem yet, but I would be talking with Jessa about other things I could do for my ankle when we had a moment alone.

"No, Mia. It's not okay. You should get a doctor to look at it. At the very least, stay off of it." He shot me a look that said he wasn't kidding.

I slumped in the passenger seat, staring out the side window. "I just need a few days to heal."

"Which you're not getting by going to work." Ethan rubbed my leg near the knee. "Come on, babe. Don't do this to yourself. You should R.I.C.E." Rest, ice, compress, elevate. I knew all of that. His hand slid a little further up my leg but stopped. Argh. I wouldn't let myself get sidetracked from the argument. No, just a discussion.

"I will be fine. I know what I'm doing. Plus if it doesn't feel better, I promise I'll see a doctor." I ran a hand through my hair and stared out the window, not looking in his direction because I knew he wouldn't take the promise seriously. He knew how I was. I trusted magic and herbs over doctors. Besides, they'd proven a more powerful and healthy way to handle any ailments, except I was getting in the way of the healing process.

"If you don't keep your promise, I'll have to tell your parents. You know they'll be upset that you haven't seen a doctor." Humor softened his voice, and it was the only thing keeping me from pummeling my fists against his chest. If he told my parents, they would force me into being seen; they would nag until I did.

"I already told Nolan, so don't worry. You'll probably have competition over who tells first." I grumbled, sliding further in the seat. I hadn't realized that Nolan might tell, if not in passing. At least he didn't know how serious my foot was. He only knew I'd asked for his help because I hadn't been comfortable with driving.

"What?" Ethan's voice dropped to a gravely growl. "You went to him first?"

Oh boy, this was just my luck. I wish I hadn't brought up my brother. I should've kept my mouth shut. "Yes, I asked him because I didn't want to—"

"You didn't want to bother me? Or you weren't comfortable asking me because of the problems we had?" He pulled into a parking spot at the hospital and turned off the ignition. His fingers bit into my leg just above the knee.

I reluctantly looked at him, knowing he wanted me to. "Fine. You're right. I didn't ask you because of the problems we've been having. I don't know how to handle you as a werewolf." My heart pounded in my ears, and I wiped sweaty palms on my skirt. "I'm scared. I know the werewolves don't like me, and I'm afraid when you become one of them you'll feel the same way. I don't want them to take you away from me."

He stared at me, his eyes were stony at first, but they melted into a look of sadness. "Mia, babe, you have to know how that sounds. I wouldn't leave you for the world." Something in his eyes shifted before he forced his emotions in check. "You mean more to me than the Pack. We're meant to be together. Nothing will stop that." He brushed his thumb over my cheek. "Let's get your friend safely home. We'll talk more about this a bit later."

I nodded, knowing I was probably overreacting. I couldn't help it, realizing he was becoming more werewolf. He meant everything he said, but how could he hold to his word? The wolves held a lot of power over Chad, so it made sense that they would do the same with Ethan since he was a lower rank. I wasn't stupid.

He leaned in pressing a sweet and tender kiss on my lips, but I burned for so much more.

*T*ension radiated from the backseat of Ethan's car. Ever since we walked in, Jessa narrowed her eyes at me, but she didn't say much. The silence bothered me more than her getting upset. Maybe I should've let Nolan call one of his friends.

No, I wouldn't second guess myself.

"How are you feeling, Jessa?" Ethan asked, trying to break the awkward silence.

"I'm fine. Thank you." She kept her hands in her lap and sat with a ramrod posture. I looked away, not wanting to meet her gaze again. "Turn right at the next street."

Ethan did as she requested.

I stifled a groan. My hopes of talking with her about my ankle would have to wait. She wouldn't be willing to talk, not with the way she was acting.

"I don't think Mia should go to the shop for a few days," Ethan said, glancing in the rearview mirror.

I couldn't believe him. "What?"

"Your ankle. You need to rest."

I opened my mouth to argue, but he cut me a look that said he didn't want to hear it.

"If you can't drive to pick up Jessa, then I don't see how you'd drive to the shop. Much less having to deal with customers and whatever else needs to be done." Ethan returned his gaze to Jessa in the rearview mirror.

I turned in my seat a little, but even that movement hurt my ankle a little. I frowned at her. "It's fine. I can watch over the shop for a few more days since I know you still need to recover. The doctor said he wanted you to rest, so I know you're not up to going back to the store yet."

She frowned at me then looked at Ethan. She wasn't exactly a fan of his, but she didn't dislike him as strongly as she'd detested Greg, which was an improvement. The only problem she had with Ethan—at least that I knew of—was that he would become a werewolf. Since Jared had attacked her, she hated all werewolves. She didn't want to hear that Chad and Ethan had helped rescue her; even though Chad pissed me off, he knew I wasn't a bad person.

"I know you're trying to look out for her, but I need Mia's help with the shop." Jessa just looked sad. "If I was in better shape, I would agree that she should be home resting, but unfortunately that's not the case." She stared at me, meeting my gaze. "I'll go in and get you something that should help with the swelling."

What would she give me that I couldn't get from the shop? "I already used the comfrey poultice and tried a potion for the pain."

Ethan appeared both parts curious and skeptical; then again, a few weeks ago I wouldn't have even broached this subject with him in the car.

Jessa didn't look too comfortable with him here either, but she was more open about magic than I was. Plus, we knew he would soon be something more dangerous to society than us. We were real witches, but witches were nothing compared to werewolves on the hunt. At least when it came to the magic I knew about. I'm pretty sure black magic witches were capable of truly horrific things, but that wasn't on my radar, so far at least.

"What I'll give you is stronger than that, but it'll be fine. My recipe is written down at home." She looked between Ethan and me again. "You can read over it."

73

"Thanks, Jessa." I gave a small smile, even though I felt so awkward being here with her and Ethan at the same time. I just wished we wouldn't have had to go through this conversation.

"Keep off the leg as much as possible." Jessa shrugged. "It's fine if you can't do the normal cleaning routine, as long as nothing looks too dusty or dirty. It can go a few days until one of us is feeling better."

"Yeah, don't overdo it, babe." Ethan made another turn onto the road that lead closer toward where Jessa lived.

At least the car trip was slowly going better. I hadn't liked the way it started with both of them going after me for my ankle. At least Ethan hadn't gotten around to truly scolding me for jumping out the window yet. Maybe he'd forgotten. From the look on his face, I doubted he did. I bet this conversation had reignited the idea, but I'd deal with them and their concerns. It was nice knowing they cared.

"I know my limits." I settled back into the passenger seat, and Ethan slid his hand into mine. I wasn't sure if it was only for my benefit or to show a united force in front of Jessa, but I was sure he would've done it regardless because he knew I was uncomfortable.

"I know you do. We care. That's all." Ethan stroked his thumb over the top of my hand.

"Thanks."

"There's a stool in the back of the shop that I use sometimes to get up to the higher shelves; you can prop your foot on it," Jessa piped up. "If you need help finding it, call me tomorrow." Her tone had normalized a little, becoming less grumpy and more like the friend who was always there for me. Definitely more than a certain brother who would rather get it on with his latest girlfriend than take me to pick up my best friend.

"I will." I smiled back at her. "Thank you."

Ethan squeezed my hand a little. "I'll take you before I go in. You'll be there earlier than you'd probably want to be, but at least you won't have to drive."

I wasn't looking forward to waking up at his ungodly hours. One of the things I liked about working at Jessa's shop was that she opened at a reasonable time. I didn't need to be awake before the sun climbed into the sky. However, for the next few days, it looked like that would change.

I groaned, rubbing my other hand over his. "I guess I'll need to pack my e-reader."

Ethan chuckled, the low sound caressing my body. "Guess so. You'll probably be bored out of your mind waking up so early."

"At least it's better than driving with my foot like this." Maybe I could look through some magic books.

I wouldn't bring my grandmother's grimoire with me out in public, especially not to Eternally Magick when Selene could come back. If any other witch found out it was on me, they might steal it for themselves and soak up the knowledge within, making themselves much more powerful. So much knowledge had been passed through the generations; to lose it would be horrendous.

I had thought about having the grimoire digitized since then I would know it was safe, no matter if there was a fire or whatever else. However, I hadn't gotten around to it. The tome was huge and filled with so many ancient pages.

"If you need something to read, I have plenty of books in my office." I knew Jessa meant the werewolf book. I'd been weaker then. Now I wasn't. I knew what was good for me without having to look to Jessa for approval.

"That's fine. I already have a few books I'm interested in."

We slipped back into silence while Ethan drove. Within no time, we were at Jessa's place. I remained in the car while Ethan walked with Jessa to the door. She said a few things to him, but from how he acted, I knew she hadn't said anything offensive, probably just that she'd get whatever potion she had for me inside while he waited on her door step.

Great going, Jessa.

I rolled my eyes, wishing I'd gone home and used the rest of the salve I'd made. Even though it had a little of the love potion I had been affected by before. But it was tied to Ethan, and we were together, so I didn't see how it would be a problem.

But it was about time I pitched the stuff and made a new, untainted batch. If I did use it and it backfired again, I wouldn't survive it. I refused to have my relationship with Ethan go the way things went with Greg.

Ethan came back to the car with a small plastic grocery bag. "Here you go."

"Thanks. I really mean it." By the time I looked back to Jessa's house, she had already shut the front door. The lacey white curtains moved a little, but they soon fell back into place.

Sighing, I tried not to feel disappointed when it came to Jessa's behavior. For a moment, I'd thought we were past that, but now I didn't know.

"Where to now?" Ethan asked. "Have you eaten yet?"

"Yes," I said, looking him over. His stomach grumbled. "Have you?"

"I did earlier with Nolan, but I'm hungry again." He gave me a wicked grin. "Although, there's something delicious sitting beside me."

My body felt like it burst into flames at the comment, and the temperature in the car ratchet up at least ten degrees. "You're not the only one feeling that way." I tried to remind myself we needed to talk, not fall into bed and rut like bunnies all night long. We needed to figure out what was going on with one another. Or at least I had to know what was happening with him and the Pack before we went to bed together.

"Good. Let's head to your house." Sizzling sensuality from his voice made my thighs wet. "Nolan may or may not be home tonight."

I wouldn't give my thoughts on that subject since from what I'd heard, I was pretty sure Nolan would be spending the night. The two of them were almost as bad as Ethan and I.

Jessa lived on the other side of our medium-sized town, closer to the shop than where my family, Ethan, and I lived.

The trip home seemed to take forever.

MIA

*M*y quaint house towered over us, whispering what was undoubtedly going to happen once we stepped inside. I relished the anticipation that coursed through me.

Ethan slid his hot palm ever higher on my thigh. His hand trembled with pent-up sexual frustration.

I could relate.

He pulled away, getting the keys from the ignition before striding to the passenger side. He opened the car door for me, but I wasn't sure how I'd get out since easing myself into the vehicle had been painful enough. Now I'd have to position myself carefully to climb out. I wasn't looking forward to this, but only a little bit further and I'd be able to lie in bed with Ethan and relax my ankle. I couldn't wait.

Ethan slid his hands underneath me. Before I realized what he was doing, he lifted me from the car. I wrapped my arms around his neck, savoring the closeness. He used the car remote to lock it while he carried me to the front door. I unlocked it with a little struggle before we were finally inside.

The older lady who lived next door had something else to talk with her friends about now. These days she wasn't quite so obvious with her spying, but she was still as nosy as ever.

That was the one bad point about living in my grandparents' former home. However, I liked not having to pay rent. Besides, my grandmother had left it to me in her will, along with the grimoire, which she'd kept in a special compartment in the spare bedroom. The same place I kept it when I wasn't actively using it.

No one else knew where I hid it, and that's exactly how I'd like to keep it.

Ethan set me on the couch. "Rest here for a moment. Let me help you with your shoes, and I'll take mine off before we head upstairs." He bent beside me. I wanted to run my hands through his soft hair and down his hardened jawline. He was so incredibly handsome. I couldn't help loving him.

"Thank you." I had opted for strappy sandals, since wearing tennis shoes with the swollen ankle was something I'd wanted to avoid. His hands brushed my foot as he unbuckled the sandals. "Is there anything you're concerned about with the Pack that you haven't told me? At least anything important?"

He snatched my sandals from the floor and stood, but his gaze remained lowered avoiding my eyes. There was something on his mind, but I wasn't sure if I wanted to know what it was. Maybe I could take the question back before the subject got too serious.

"You deserve to know. I'm not thrilled about this, and I will fight it if I can. The Pack wants me with a female werewolf." He shifted his attention to the ceiling. His breathing came out slow and steady as if he was trying to keep himself under control.

Lightheadedness washed over me and tears burned my eyes.

The Pack was crazy. They couldn't do this to us. Chad hadn't mentioned any of this. Why hadn't Ethan told me sooner? I couldn't lose Ethan to the wolves, not like this. My fears were coming to pass. I'd hoped I wouldn't lose him to the Pack, but now I might be doing just that and for an entirely different reason.

"H-how long have you known?" The words didn't even sound like my own voice had spoken them.

"Not long. I found out last night." He knelt at my side again. "I didn't want to tell you before I had a chance to talk to Chad and fight this. No matter what, I won't let them split us apart."

I nodded, but I wasn't confident that he could make much of a difference when it came to fighting the will of the Pack. Their Alpha's authority wasn't something to be questioned, or at least that's what I'd read in the werewolf book. I only hoped Ethan didn't try too hard and end up getting himself hurt or killed. I'd rather have him alive and with a girl werewolf than dead.

"We could run away if I'm not able to work things out with them. They can't have infinite reach."

He tilted my chin up so I'd look at him.

"They don't need infinite reach. Other Packs out there will have their own ways of doing things. You never know how bad they'll be. At least Chad seems interested in helping you, while the Pack thought about killing you. If that's how this group is, how will another group be?" I leaned back on the couch. Part of me wanted to throw a blanket over my face and disappear, but hiding wasn't the answer to this.

"It's going to be okay. We're going to work through it. I'll figure out how I can get them to pay attention to what I need. Chad said if I help them with a missing person, I could leverage some influence with the Alpha. He might be more interested then in my desires than dictating to me."

Ethan brushed his lips over mine, but the kiss spoke his frustration more than simply showing passion. He ran his hand over my side, from my shoulder all the way down to my hip.

I wanted to curl into his warmth and wrap myself in him. He was safe and if I had to, I would reassert my own power to the Pack. They might not like me, but I had enough belief in our relationship that I wouldn't let the werewolves stomp all over me. They didn't know I was closer to a novice than most witches.

Besides, I'd charred their former second in command and almost killed their Alpha, even though that last part had been a complete and utter accident.

"I know we will." I trailed my hands over his torso.

He dropped my shoes beside the couch and bent closer, pulling me into his arms, once again taking the utmost care not to hurt my swollen ankle. He lifted me into his arms, then hastily kicked off his shoes before walking upstairs with me.

When we finally got to my bedroom, he laid me in the center of the bed before crawling on too. I was ready for his love and happy he'd told me the truth about the werewolves wanting him with a female wolf, even if it cut me to the core.

Honesty was something we could work with. If I didn't know what was going on, then it felt like he was withdrawing to protect a dark secret.

I moved a little under his firm body. My foot brushed against his leg and pain radiated out from my ankle. I grimaced before I could hold it in.

"Are you okay, babe?" He glanced down the length of my body. "Here, let me make sure you're comfortable before we even think about going forward with this."

Ethan never failed to surprise me. He took such wonderful care of me while I was hurt that it made me want to do whatever I could to be there for him too. How could I have ever questioned him?

I wanted to bathe him in love and lust until neither of us could walk straight. "I'm okay. Just brushed my foot against your leg on accident. I should've been more careful."

He grabbed one of the pillows and carried it to the end of the bed, where he very gently propped my foot up. "This should help a bit. At least you'll be able to relax a little more and your foot would be in the best position to heal." He trailed his palm over my shin, then he slid it up to my thighs. The path his hand traveled left behind fire and pleasure, and I wanted to close my eyes and sink into the wonderful feelings caressing me.

"You're right. This feels so much better." I grinned at him, unable to help myself. "You're very good."

He winked and slid onto the bed next to me, propping his head on his palm. "If you need more proof on how good I am, let me know." He leaned in and gave me a lingering kiss. "I wouldn't want to pressure you into anything you're not comfortable with." His words were the only sign that he was willing to stop right here. Everything else made him look like a predator ready to pounce its prey.

The worst thing was instinctively I knew this must be his beast coming to the surface, yet I still wanted him inside of me. I didn't care about the fact werewolves scared me, or that he was slowly becoming one. Right now, he was Ethan and that was all that mattered.

"I don't feel pressured into anything. Don't push me away. I know you can smell how much I want you." I caressed his cheek with my fingertips, closing the distance between us again.

His soft lips brushed mine, slowly at first. The press of his tongue demanded access to my mouth. I opened for him, letting him taste me and claim me as I wanted him to do with my body, which for the moment was slow but steady. We both enjoyed sex harder and wilder, but that wouldn't go down well with my ankle like this.

He caressed his hand over my body and along my curves before he slid to the button on my skirt. Pulling away from the kiss, he unfastened it. I didn't mind because I wanted both of us to be naked. "Let me get this off you. Lift your hips if you can, baby. I'll do the rest."

I arched into the air as much as I could, and he slipped the skirt off. Biting my lower lip, I enjoyed this shared moment. Even though Ethan was becoming a werewolf, he was still the man I loved. He loved me and accepted me, and that was a lot more than Greg had offered.

"Is everything okay, Mia?" he asked, worry sliding into his voice. "I'm not hurting you, am I?" He stopped what he was doing, but I kept my hips up, wanting him get the skirt off. He hooked his thumb into my dainty panties, taking them away as well.

"I'm not hurting. It's fine." I smiled, but from the look in his eyes, he knew there was something wrong. But I refused to tell him I'd just thought of how shitty my ex had been while making love to him. That really wouldn't sit right, not with him or with me.

Seconds ticked by and I wondered if he'd take my avoidance and drop it. And he did.

When he looked back up my body, the agitation had faded from his eyes and he looked wilder and hungrier than before. He nibbled on my leg near my knee, then moved the pillow my foot was propped on so my legs were spread.

I bit my lower lip, wanting to feel his mouth on me. With Ethan in charge, I'd be able to lay back and relish in the delicious torment he drew out of my body when he caressed me with his tongue without worrying about my ankle, even if I'd rather be straddling him.

He nibbled along the inside of my thigh as he carefully crawled between my legs. He lifted my shirt, exposing my stomach and smooth satin bra. His fingertips brushed over the material.

I moaned, enjoying the fact Ethan so clearly savored my body and what he wanted to do to me. He was like a man with a mission, and his mission was my pleasure. Whatever he did was so I'd reach bliss. The fact he dominated and sometimes got wilder and rougher just made these moments much more fun and intense. Of course, I liked being in charge sometimes, but I loved submitting to Ethan's will while we were in the bedroom.

He slid his lips over my thigh toward my folds, and I spread my uninjured leg wider wanting all he had to offer, both his tongue and his solid erection.

He traced his tongue over my lips before slipping between them. With the hand that wasn't playing with my breasts, he nudged a finger against my entrance. He probed my core, allowing time for me to adjust before thrusting his digit in and out faster.

I groaned, tilting my head back and staring up at the ceiling. My life was more complete than it had ever been, yet so many things battled me for the small victories I'd won. But I needed to take each day as it came instead of beating myself up for past missteps. Doing that would help no one.

I slid my hands through his short hair, focusing on the sweet sensations tugging between my legs as he circled his tongue over my clit, caressing it in delightful strokes as pleasure buzzed through me.

Arching my back, I placed my hand over his. "Ethan," I moaned. The t-shirt and bra had to come off. I wanted the press of our nude bodies together. His touch electrified and soothed all at the same time.

He slid his gaze up the length of my body, and he had a

relaxed if not slightly feral look in his eyes. The look drew more wetness between my legs and I spread them ever farther. He added another finger to the mix, and I gasped. Pleasure intensified within me.

I wanted so much more, but this was really what I'd needed. With everything going on recently, reconnecting with Ethan was more important than I'd realized. We'd come this far. Nolan, Jessa, all the werewolf stuff; those things would resolve themselves.

He thrust his fingers in deeper and faster, bringing me ever closer to the edge. I bit my lower lip. "Oh goodness, Ethan... You're amazing."

Ethan chuckled. The husky rumbling sound reverberated through my body and sent shivers chasing up my spine. He did this on purpose. He had to know how much all of this turned me on. That was the reason he was so confident and sexy, right?

"I want you inside me. Please." He wasn't even naked, but I just couldn't imagine not having him in me.

He winked. "Patience, my love."

My body burned. If he didn't do something, I would be flying into the arms of a climax before he even took his shirt off. Or maybe that was the point.

He removed his fingers from me, and my body felt empty without him. I glanced down, but I didn't have much chance because his tongue slid lower delving inside my core and searing me with desire.

I gripped his short hair, wishing for a moment it were a little longer. "Oh, oh, my goodness. Don't stop." Lust toyed with me. Climax grew ever closer, remaining just out of reach but not by much.

He thrust his tongue within me, licking with nearly ravishing strokes of his tongue like a starving man.

The orgasm hit me like a ton of bricks and I cried out. My

body shattered as waves of pleasure crashed over me again and again.

Ethan continued teasing me until I was pretty sure I would have nothing left for him. I panted and blinked up at the ceiling, feeling drained and boneless.

What had I ever done to get such a wonderful guy in my life? Oh, that's right. I'd made a love potion that screwed with my karma, but ultimately I'd won over the man of my dreams.

Pulling back, he grinned at me. "Now that I've got you how I want you." He hopped off the bed with such agility that I'd have thought he was some kind of feline shifter. It unnerved me a little, but I brushed it off. He was a soldier, so he was more athletic than most. It only made sense that he was acquiescing to his supernatural abilities like that.

He slid a condom from the pack in my bedside nightstand before he unbuckled his belt and unzipped his pants. He did it slowly and kept his gaze on me, letting me know exactly how erotically charged he was. I wanted him so much, much more than I'd ever imagined even during my terribly horny teenage years.

My desire for him was one of the reasons why I hadn't really dated much. My parents had thought I was some sweet good girl who was holding off for the right guy and doing as they told me. They hadn't really wanted me to date until I was at least eighteen, but I'd known better. I had a few boyfriends, but nothing that had been too serious.

In college, on the other hand, when I pretty well knew any chance of Ethan ever acknowledging my existence was next to nil had been a whole 'nother story. I may have gone wild but I wasn't too bad. Some of my college friends had been *a lot* worse.

After my grandmother passed away, I'd withdrawn from socializing, so those friends were long gone. Most of them had moved away where there were better jobs and better pay. More opportunities.

Not me.

I'd still hoped to catch Ethan's eye, but when he'd been deployed, my heart had hurt. I'd worried I might never see him again. Watching the news to see what was going on in the Middle East hadn't soothed my fears, but he'd sent the occasional email to Nolan and made the rare phone call. When that happened, my brother made sure to give my family updates about Ethan's well-being, so I'd known he was okay.

Ethan dropped his jeans to the floor. He wasn't wearing any underwear, and I loved knowing he was so excited that we were about to be intimate. He tugged his shirt off, causing his sculpted muscles to flex.

Small beads of sweat formed on my skin. He rolled the condom on his thick, long cock, and I marveled at the sight. I couldn't help it. I enjoyed being with him, and he knew what he was doing, which made the bouts of romance that much sweeter. He somehow always manipulated my body into doing exactly as he pleased.

He crawled onto the bed and nudged my legs further apart. He helped me up enough to pull my shirt over my head and unhook my bra. The feel of our bodies, skin on skin, was delightful. He pressed me down on the bed and I ran my hands over his chest, kissing him on the lips.

The tip of his cock nudged at my entrance and I arched my back, wanting to push him inside of me and have him fill my body. But he wasn't about to let me take his thunder, even though I knew he was more than ready for me. "Just relax. Let me do the heavy lifting." He nibbled a path down my neck. "I want to make you scream my name. Let's give your neighbor something to gossip about."

"If she isn't too hard of hearing."

"That's why screaming might be necessary to get the point…" He thrust in a little, driving himself inside me. "…Across to her."

While it sounded like a good idea, I wasn't sure how I felt about trying to annoy my neighbor. If my brother or parents came by, I didn't want the noisy old biddy to say something that would make them second-guess me, especially if she used any descriptor words like 'Army' or 'soldier.' We'd be royally screwed and the gig would be up about our relationship.

I only hoped that when the news did come out eventually, everyone would try to be happy for us rather than having their own agenda for our lives, which knowing my family was kind of a stretch.

He pushed his cock completely inside me, filling me up… stretching my body until it molded to his like a glove.

I wrapped my arms around his neck, biting my nails into his flesh and enjoying the pleasure of being this close to him.

"I love the way you feel," he murmured against my lips.

When I'd accommodated to his size, he began a steady rhythm with his hips, thrusting in and out of me with such restrained gentleness that it made me want to smack him over the head. I had a sprained ankle, but I wasn't made of glass. I wouldn't break if he took me with the way we both needed him to.

"Take me. Ravish me," I whispered. "Love me."

He pulled away, just enough to look into my eyes. Whatever he saw in them gave him the answer he searched for. He sat up and grabbed my legs by the calves, then slammed into me with a pace and strength that had me clutching the headboard.

My body ached and warmth caressed my womb, even though he'd sapped my strength with the earlier orgasm. My breath came out in harsh pants, and even though my ankle was jostled a little, sending pain through me, I didn't care.

The pain barely registered in my hypersensitive body. If anything, it added to my insatiable need for more.

He stared at me, watching the emotions flicker across my face. One minute his eyes were their normal gunmetal blue, the next they were wolf amber.

I gasped at the sudden shift. My core clenched, and before I could react in fear, climax overtook all thoughts and reason. A scream of pleasure ripped from my lips, and I smacked my hand over my mouth, moaning as my body erupted with pleasure.

Ethan groaned over me, the sound gravely and guttural as orgasm claimed him too. He teetered like he was near collapse, but he set my foot back on the pillow, before heading off to the bathroom to clean up.

My intention not to scream was ruined, but I didn't mind. I loved knowing the depth of control he had over my body.

MIA

*D*arkness blanketed the street. With it being so God-awful early, there was hardly anyone else around, so we had no problem with finding a parking spot in front of Eternally Magick.

"Just a moment, let me come around and help you out," Ethan said.

Sighing once he left the car, I knew he was trying to help, but it was coming across a bit as if he thought I would fall apart at the slightest bump. After the amazing sex last night, he'd asked a few times if my ankle was okay. Not exactly the kind of pillow talk I'd hoped for.

Besides, the salve Jessa had given me was really good. I couldn't believe how well it was working. But I'd do as Ethan said, for the most part, because I didn't want to draw out the healing process even more. I was happy he had offered to drive me to work, but this was way too early for my brain to function properly, especially after all the sexual energy expended last night.

I had no idea how Ethan did it. He looked eager to get the day started, no problem whatsoever. Then again, with all the time he'd spent in the Army, he was probably more of a morning person than I'd realized.

He opened my car door and lifted me out into the crisp morning air.

I pushed at his chest a little and glanced around to confirm the lack of people. Okay, there wasn't anyone to see him carry me around, but it did make me feel a little self-conscious.

He leveled a stern stare at me. "Don't do that. I just want to help, babe. You shouldn't be walking on it." He shut the car door behind us, then walked to the store. I carefully unlocked the door before he pushed it open. He glanced around the shop, assessing it in a similar way to how Chad had when he'd last been here.

Huh.

"You cleaned it up nicely. There were a lot of broken shelves and statues when I was last in here." He remained in the entrance for a heartbeat, before heading to the counter. His gaze slid over me, sending a familiar heat through my body.

I licked my lips and leaned into him for a kiss. He tightened his grip on me and I basked in his touch.

He pulled back a little and our eyes met. "If I didn't have to be at the base soon, I would be finding a spot where I could make love to you."

"There's a stool over there behind the counter. Or there's Jessa's office." I winked at him, wishing the same. Glass windows lined the front of the shop, so if he did take me here, we would likely be caught. Then again, there wasn't anyone around.

"Seductress." His lips brushed over mine, and he lightly tugged at my lower lip with his teeth. "Remember to stay off your foot if you can." He set me on the stool, then went into the back room.

My heart skipped a beat. Jessa only allowed me back there. If she knew he'd gone in there, she'd be furious.

I opened my mouth to protest, but he came back with the stepstool Jessa had mentioned. I let out a calming breath. Of course, he was getting the stool. I'd almost forgotten about it. Dang, he was so sweet.

"Do you need anything else while I'm here?" His gaze scanned the shop. "Oh, wait, I have something for you." He strode out of the store, and I faintly heard the slam of a car door. The store's chiming bell alerted me to his presence again. He carried a pair of crutches.

At first I wondered where he'd gotten those, especially when we'd spent most of the evening and morning together. But the scuff marks on the beige rubber pads gave them away. They had to be Nolan's from when he was a preteen. He'd broken his foot playing soccer, so he'd had to sit out the rest of the season and use a pair of crutches he resented.

Mom had caught him not using them a few times, so Dad had grounded him from playing with the Xbox. That meant he'd actually been on top of his classes and his grades were great, until he went right on back to playing too many video games again.

Yet Mom and Dad had hope.

Unlike me, I did great in school, but I always felt overlooked as if I was cursed to be invisible.

Shaking away the thoughts, I started to get up to get the crutches from Ethan, but he gave me a look that kept me on the stool with my foot propped on the stepstool. Although, I had a feeling sitting like this would probably get uncomfortable fast.

"Nolan's old crutches. I grabbed them from the garage while getting ready this morning. If you do need to get up, you should use these. They might not be the most comfortable, but we can see about getting you some different ones later." Now it was my turn to give dirty stares. "If you're not doing any better."

I loved that he cared this much about me, even if he was fussing over me more than I'd prefer. Just like a mother hen. I smiled, keeping that thought to myself. Somehow, I didn't think this hunky military man would appreciate the comparison. "Thanks. I'd forgotten about Nolan's crutches. They'll be better than nothing, I guess."

He leaned them against the counter beside me, and I stretched to get one last kiss from him. I couldn't help it.

"When does the shop close?" He looked toward the door, but the sign with the hours wasn't visible from this spot.

"The store closes at seven. So I'll probably be ready about fifteen minutes after that."

"Okay, I'll come straight over after work," he said. "That way if you need any help with sweeping or closing up, I'll be here." He pressed one last kiss on my forehead.

I groaned. That meant he'd be standing around for about an hour, but knowing Ethan, he'd probably head over as soon as he could. "You don't need to do that, but I appreciate it."

"No problem. Have a great day, babe. Love you." With that, he walked out.

"Love you too!" I half-shouted to him, knowing he could hear me.

His car started, and I heard him pull away from the curb.

Sighing, I stared at my ankle then around at the really quiet shop. Eternally Magick didn't open for a couple hours, and I'd need to lock it up so no one would come in before then. The silence unnerved me. At least when the store was open, there were people walking, cars being driven, the occasional customer waltzing in, sunlight shining through the window. There was none of that now.

I pulled out my phone and played one of my dubstep playlists. Having some sound wouldn't make me feel quite so nervous since while I knew I was safe, there was the unforgettable memory of finding an injured Jessa on the floor. I glanced back at the exact spot and noticed a few specks of red I hadn't seen before. Blood. I'd been so careful when cleaning. Normally, I probably wouldn't have even paid any attention to the tiny drops.

With my foot in the shape it was, I didn't think scrubbing the floors was in my future. However, I found it hard to look away from the spot. I'd get to it, or maybe Ethan could help me when he got off work. Or I'd put it off for a few days, fingers crossed, when my foot was doing better.

I grabbed the crutches and gingerly lifted my foot off the stool. Something strange set me on edge. I'd never felt anything quite like this before. I hobbled toward the front door with my keys in hand.

With the door locked, I turned to see Selene standing there. I dropped the keys, confusion weighed on my chest. The bell on the door hadn't gone off to alert me of anyone entering the shop. Plus, I'd been sitting right there.

She stared expectantly at me as if she'd been waiting for me to notice her. "Well, have you thought about my offer to help you?"

I leaned the crutches against a shelf, then backed away a few steps from Selene. Fear skittered around in my stomach like creeping crawling things. Why hadn't I heard her?

"Mia, it's impolite to not answer when someone's talking to you." She strode toward me with that feline grace.

My mouth opened and closed as words tried to form in my throat, but I couldn't speak, couldn't think. I took another step away and my back bumped a wall.

She stopped in front of me, extending her hand with its red claw-like fingernails. She scraped one of them over my cheek, from my eyebrow down to my lips, then she slid it down over my lower lip, closing in until I was sure she would kiss me.

"I need more time." The words rushed from my mouth, causing our lips to barely brush.

Rolling her eyes, she leaned back just a little. "There's not much time left. Sooner than later, I'll need a response. Don't let Jessa stand in the way of you becoming all your grandmother wanted you to be. You wouldn't want to disappoint Rose, would you?"

I squeezed my eyes shut, hating the uncertainty running through me. Selene was trying to make me second-guess Jessa. But the way Jessa had reacted to my mentioning the other witch made a tiny part of me wonder if there was a grain of truth to Selene's words.

I opened my eyes to respond. But Selene was gone.

13

ETHAN

*T*he checkpoint had the same uneasy feeling as yesterday. Security was usually strict but flowing easily. Now it was sluggish and stressful. Even the gate seemed to struggle when it rose, as if hesitant to let me back on base.

Rookies ran a lap along a trail most of us knew like the backs of our hands. At least they seemed oblivious to the tension building around them. My wolf circled inside my head, constantly on alert due to the uneasy feeling in the air. A few sergeants I passed focused on a movie discussion, but their hearts weren't in it. No usual puns or bad jokes.

My thoughts turned increasingly broody. I didn't notice at first, but my upper lip had inched up baring my teeth; the wolf wanted to growl his frustration. I needed to regain some control. If I'd had space, I would've gone running, but the time spent helping Mia had made that impossible.

Before reaching the office, I cooled down enough to loosen the worst signs of the wolf's anxiety. It wasn't so much the baring of the teeth, but the minute differences one might look for. My nostrils flared, taking in the scents, and my ears ached with the need to catch every faint whisper to warn me of an oncoming attack. I still had a lot to learn from Chad.

The office was quiet. Some of the morning duties were suspended until further notice. My lieutenant simply directed me to stay nearby until further notice, with gear on. My spine tingled, adrenaline flowing through my system.

Preparation for battle was easy, the actual wait and readiness was tense. The routine of putting my gear on took my mind away from the furry aspect of my life. This was familiar; this was known and good.

Within minutes, the rest of the squad gathered around. Each took only a moment to greet one another before starting their dance with the equipment.

We sat together for half an hour, not saying much other than a whisper here or there. Our captain arrived with a small leather briefcase cuffed around his left wrist. One by one, he and the lieutenant called us into an adjoining room. It wasn't long before it was my turn. I headed to the room and stood at attention.

"Sit down, Ethan. Let's be brief. There is a situation taking place that is escalating quickly. To contain it, we've been requested to provide some manpower. What I'm asking is that you read over these documents. Once they're signed, you'll be transported to a site where you'll be properly briefed," the captain noted evenly. His eyes were stern and voice grave. Whatever it was had set him on edge.

I glanced through the stack of papers. "Security clearance requests, NDA's..." I lifted my gaze to him. I had served under him, and I knew the slight level of lenience he allowed his soldiers. I had a little room to be direct.

"I know. It's not usual. But like I said, we've been asked for our assistance. We don't run this operation. The request came from high up, so don't question it. They didn't tell me who is in charge. But we are called to serve," the captain said, handing over the pen.

With a few strokes of the pen, I signed the documents. The lieutenant simply opened the door, and I left the room. What was I getting myself into? The thought of calling Chad entered my mind, but I wouldn't have time to do it before we left.

Walking outside, I spotted a mercenary standing beside one of our Humvees. He wore a black uniform and had on proper gear, but it was arranged differently. Nodding to me, he simply pointed to the last vehicle. Guess they weren't paid enough for small talk.

I climbed into the last Humvee to find two of my fireteam already there. Both wore a slightly concerned look on their faces. During our deployment, the conflict, our enemy and our job had been clear. Now we didn't really even know who we were working for, or better yet, why.

The small convoy took off after a while. Questions formed in my mind, but they were quickly shattered when the driver turned on the radio. The scenery sped by to the sound of 80s hard rock music.

The off-site location we arrived at was an old warehouse. The three-brick-thick exterior was plain but sturdy with a heavy wall between the outside and us. An entrance and loading dock was defensible and easily secured. To the amazement of our squad, the office even had a small kitchenette.

Once we arrived, the atmosphere slightly relaxed. The silent mercenaries who had let us in showed us around. So far, everything seemed standard. Only when we asked about the assignment did the merc get frosty again.

I headed upstairs after a while, finding a set of lockers and an area for bedrolls. It wasn't much, but it did beat some of the places I'd had to sleep. However, I most regretted being without Mia for the remainder of the assignment. The lockers prompted me with my routine and I went to work on my gear.

Non-essentials and personal items went into the locker, leaving my backpack light and easy to carry around. I doubted I needed extra rations with me, so they stayed behind too. Here and there, the rest of the squad meandered up to check things out and prepare. Equipment maintenance, weapon oiling and cleaning, followed by ammunitions check were essential menial tasks, but we knew it was worth it. Whatever our mission would be, we'd be ready.

It wasn't until late afternoon when we were ordered downstairs. A stocky bald mercenary stood next to a slender man with glasses, who gave the standing orders. It was mostly the usual. Not telling family about the location, and no calls until after work. Absolute denial about actions and activities involving the Army onsite. Movement to onsite would be in an enclosed van to prevent knowledge of location. The list went on for a while. While we weren't on duty, things were pretty relaxed. Onsite, we were rookies again and would follow all orders without question.

Our duty was to protect the location and if needed, prevent assets from leaving there by whatever means necessary, including deadly force. No one in, unless authorized by security; no one out, except through security. No talking and no phone calls; radio silence unless otherwise stated. Meals were to be eaten off-site.

Everything seemed standard.

At least we weren't guarding an ammo dump. People I could handle. Something that might explode with little to no warning made me nervous.

The skinny man finally finished giving the orders and posted a schedule on the wall. Five overlapping six-hour shifts. It was still blank. Without hesitation, I wrote my name into the first slot and grabbed my gear. There was only a half-hour window before my shift would start. The sooner I was done, the sooner I could get out and call Mia.

I was teamed up with two newer faces—Horn and Fredricks—I hadn't spoken with either man much, and one of the mercs joined as our fourth. Looking around the room, almost everything was as it should have been. The only odd thing was the mercenaries. Still, as long as we were all on the same side, I didn't care who they were.

The front door opened, and Baldie, the silent mercenary, signaled for us to follow him. I wasn't sure if I was comfortable being ordered by signal commands only. While most disliked having a person yell at them, it usually meant they cared enough for you to not mess up. My thoughts were interrupted as Baldie held up his right fist in the air, a clear sign to stop.

Out front was a blue utility van parked by a loading ramp. The doors were open, revealing impact seats and harnesses. They needed to keep the location a closely guarded secret, so they were using refurbished vans for the job.

Were they concerned about anyone knowing the Army was involved, or did they simply have something they were hiding?

At the command from Baldie, I entered the van and sat. Once everyone was ready, the doors closed leaving us all in pitch-black darkness then a fist banged against the van twice. The engine turned, and before long, we were on our way.

14

MIA

I glanced down at my cell phone again. After the incident with Selene, I wanted Ethan here more than ever. I wouldn't allow myself to be afraid of her, but I didn't like the way she'd touched me.

Plus the way she'd come into the shop without me even hearing or seeing her approach freaked me out. If I'd had my car, I would've just left. While I could've called Jessa and told her what happened, after last night I didn't know if I wanted to deal with her.

Instead, I waited for Ethan. It was thirty minutes after he typically got off work. Normally, he might even be home by now. I knew, because I'd spent some time with Nolan before when Ethan had gotten off from work, so I had a rough idea when he arrived home.

Maybe I shouldn't be getting too crazy. Something might've come up, but I couldn't help the fear lurking in my chest. I'd checked my phone for any news, and I didn't see anything about incidents at the base or large traffic accidents. Still, he could've had a report or mission he needed to do, and the shop wasn't closed yet. I still had about an hour to go.

I ran my hand through my hair, taking a few more deep breaths. *Keep calm. Keep calm. It'll be okay.*

Time ticked by so slowly, and I browsed the web on my phone knowing I'd never get back to the book I was reading. Knowing Ethan wasn't here when he should've been put me on edge.

Online women's articles on 'How to be a Better Lover' weren't exactly what I needed either, because those reminded me of Ethan too.

Finally, I pulled up my email, deciding I'd sort through it and keep an eye on my cell phone's clock every few minutes. After about an hour, there was still no sign of Ethan, and now I was freaked.

My heart raced. I positioned the crutches under my armpits and hobbled to the door. But I didn't see him anywhere. What should I do? Even if Jessa wanted to help me, she couldn't.

She was worse off than me, and she wasn't happy about me being with Ethan in the first place. She might mouth off that he could have given into his wild side and run away, or whatever else.

I thought about stepping outside and walking around to see if he'd just parked out there so as not to bother me. But I couldn't leave the shop unattended.

No, I doubted he'd just sit in the car while I was in here. He'd told me he would be here. My mind rolled out different scenarios, and I bit my lower lip. Unless the Pack had called another one of their crazy meetings. He'd been off to one the other night after I'd dropped by at Nolan's, so it was possible he'd been summoned to another. Wouldn't he have said something? Like he'd be late?

I called his cell phone. He couldn't take calls at work—but

he wasn't supposed to be on base right now. Besides, I needed to know.

His phone went straight to voicemail. "Ethan, where are you? I'm worried. You'd said you would be here when you got off work, and now the shop is closing. Please call me."

I'd give him five minutes while I did a little bit of tidying up, but then I needed to call someone else like... Chad. He'd know if the Pack had an emergency meeting planned. But I'd still need a ride home.

My brother better not decide to be a lazy jerk and ditch me for his girlfriend again, because that would leave Mom and Dad, and I didn't want them to give me a lift.

Unless I asked Chad... but, just, *no*.

After I'd gotten everything ready for the morning, I grimaced at the fact nearly fifteen minutes had gone by and still no word from Ethan.

My heart sank in my chest. Oh, no. I couldn't handle this anymore. I needed to know what was happening. I couldn't just sit back and wonder whether he was all right, or if he'd been in a car accident. Maybe I should've been checking with the local hospitals instead of cleaning up the shop.

No, he was almost a werewolf, and werewolves were resilient.

I dialed Chad's number, hoping he'd pick up, even though I wasn't sure whether he'd do so if he saw my number. However, he answered on the first ring.

"Yeah?" he said, sounding sleepy as if I'd just awoken him from a nap.

"Chad, have you heard from Ethan?" I wouldn't sugarcoat this. I didn't want to chitchat, not after our last conversation. He'd intimidated me, and I wouldn't take any crap from him, not when I needed his help.

"I'm not his babysitter. You're probably not happy with the female werewolf thing, but you two need to work that out." Metal clanged in the background, and he grunted in pain.

I huffed. "You're not understanding me here. He was supposed to pick me up from work, but he's not here. I'm worried about him."

Chad was proving to be less than useful. Maybe I should've saved my breath and just called Nolan. He might have heard from Ethan, but yet that didn't feel right to me. I found it hard to believe Ethan would contact Nolan but not me when he knew I needed him to drive me home.

"Did you try calling his cell?" Chad asked, as if I'd never think to do something like that.

I let my silence answer him.

"Fine. Let me make a couple calls, then I'll call you back. Just don't get your panties in a wad. There's probably a rational explanation for this." He sighed, and the line disconnected.

If I wasn't using my older brother's old crutches I would've been pacing the shop, but instead, I went back to the stool and sat down. My eyes were glued to the phone, ready to pounce when it started chiming out my dubstep beat.

Within a few minutes, Chad called back. "Bad news." He sounded like he didn't want to say more, but he couldn't just call back and say there was bad news without actually telling me what that was. "There's a new Pack meeting, so I'll talk to you later. Maybe I'll know more then."

"No! You're not going to do this. You can't." It didn't matter what he or any of the other wolves thought of me. What mattered was something had happened to Ethan, and if I didn't help find him... My heart hurt, and I slammed my fist against one of the bookshelves, cringing as pain shot through my hand. "I need to know what the bad news is."

"No one has heard from him, and there were some

strange murmurings going around at the base. Our contact wonders if the government is involved in a problem we're currently facing." He grunted as if upset with himself for saying that much.

Wait... didn't Ethan mention a missing person incident within the Pack?

"Pick me up. I need a ride home." Silence extended over the phone line. "Please, Chad." While I could've asked Nolan, I wanted to know what else Chad knew, and one of the best ways to do that was by talking face to face.

Then again, maybe I could get into this Pack meeting wherever it was. I had to help. I could be useful.

"Don't you have someone else who can take you?" He sighed, sounding truly frustrated.

"If I did, do you think I would be asking you?"

He groaned. The words hit their mark. "Fine, where are you?"

"I'm at the magic shop. I know you're familiar with its location since you came in the other day." I held my head up a little, happy to have at least one thing over him. "Besides, you're less stressed due to the potion I crafted. You owe me."

"How do you know I'm feeling less stressed?" He huffed, as if shaking away the thought I might be in his head. "And I paid you for the potion with a tip."

If he was still stressed, he wouldn't be taking naps this late in the day. The potion I gave him caused a person to be sleepier than normal due to its relaxing qualities. If he was taking it during the day, he'd have the desire to sleep more.

I gave a fake laugh. "Really? That's what you're going to say? You know, I have my ways of becoming a much bigger pain in the ass than I've been. You need to trust that I can help."

"Whoa, wait just a minute. I'm taking you home from work. No one said anything about you helping to find your boyfriend. You're in way over your head, girlie, especially with that limp you've got." He sneered. "Just give me twenty minutes, and I'll be there. But you're going straight home."

I sank my teeth into my lower lip as I put away my cell phone. If he thought I'd flop over and take it, then he had another thing coming. No one knew where Ethan was, but since we had a connection, I could find him.

If I'd been thinking clearly earlier, I might've tried scrying for him, but knowing he might need my help and that the werewolves didn't know where he was lit a fire inside me.

I was standing outside of Eternally Magick with the locked door when Chad pulled up.

He raised an eyebrow at me and rolled down the window. "It's not just a minor limp now. What did you do to yourself?"

I rolled my eyes, not amused by his arrogant sense of humor. "Ha ha." He could bite me... or not. I prided myself on my heritage as a witch, and I had no idea what being bitten by a werewolf would do to my magic. There was a lot more at play with me than with a normal human. No way would I ever submit myself to an Alpha like the wolves did. I was my own person, even if that meant I was mostly a loner.

Limping to the car on the crutches, I wasn't surprised Chad didn't get out of the car to help. I was a witch, not a top priority for him. I was the nuisance that nearly killed his father. Regret tugged at my chest. I put the crutches in the backseat, then slowly lowered myself into the vehicle. Once I shut the car door, I turned to him. "Take me to the Pack meeting too. I can help."

"Get out." His tone was deadly serious. He stared me straight in the eyes, seething with anger that I'd brought it up again.

I held his gaze, knowing it was stupid for me to do so. He would see it as a challenge, and honestly, I was weaker than the last time I faced down a werewolf. Maybe not magically, but if he chased, there would be no way I could run from him.

"Get out of my car. I'm not going to stand for this nonsense." Chad leaned over me, brushing his arm over my midriff as he opened the car door. His touch was like fire. He burned hot. An angry vibe of power radiated from his touch, sending a shiver down my spine. "If you keep talking like that, I'll throw you out. Do you want a ride home or not?"

"Yes, I do want a ride." I bit my tongue on where I actually wanted to go, but if he wouldn't drive me, then I would need to fight through the pain and follow him in my own car.

Chad pulled away from the curb and drove straight to my place. Instead of prying into what he'd learned, the drive was silent. "We're here."

Argh!

Maybe I needed another tactic here. Glancing over him, I cocked an eyebrow. "Could I have some help getting out? Also since you're stressed, I could give you some relaxing tea since you've been so kind."

He rested his forehead against the steering wheel. Frustration poured from him in waves of stinging energy.

My grandmother's grimoire had a recipe for a potion that might make him more agreeable. If I gave him a potent enough dose, he might allow me go to the Pack meeting. Not that I wanted to go, but if it meant I'd be able to see Ethan again, then I would do everything in my power. I wouldn't leave him to die or succumb to the danger he was in.

"Fine." Chad got out of the car, and I nearly bounced in the seat, except it would have hurt my ankle and raised suspicion. He yanked open the passenger door and stared down at me. "I can't stay long. If they discover I'm hanging out having tea with you, witch, I'll be in big trouble. You can kiss all the things I'm doing to help your boyfriend goodbye." He hefted me over his shoulder like a sack of potatoes.

A scream bubbled up in my throat and I fisted my hands in his shirt. If I'd been wearing one of my shorter skirts, my ass would've been on display for the whole neighborhood.

He also grabbed the crutches and my purse. I couldn't help but be wildly impressed by his abilities to juggle me and all of my stuff. However, his hand slid from a respectable position on my leg to one a little too close to my thighs for my comfort.

"Okay, what key is it?" he asked, as we made it to the door.

"The one with the hardware store logo on it. Next to the car key."

The keys rattled in his hands, and he unlocked the door.

The old woman from next door stepped outside to get her mail. *Oh boy.* Her gaze met mine and a look of disapproval burned on her face. *Great. Now she probably thinks I have a male harem.* Then again, she probably heard some of my screams during the lovemaking session last night.

My skin warmed with embarrassment, and I buried my face into Chad's back, even though it was the last place I'd want to be.

He closed the door behind us, then set me to the floor. His eyebrows were drawn together as if he wasn't exactly sure what to think about me plastering my face against his back, but I didn't really care. I wasn't about to explain it, and he wasn't about to ask either.

"So, what kind of tea is this?" he asked, following me into the kitchen. I was glad I hadn't moved my supplies since I'd started utilizing my magic regularly and making more potions. However, my only problem was he'd seen me dig for my magical supplies before. I didn't want him to suspect anything, so he couldn't spot me.

"It's a soothing blend I bought from a store in the mall." I nodded to the couch in the living room. "I can bring it in if you don't want to stand around and watch me boil water."

He chuckled. "You might need help." He was on to me.

I walked to the cabinet where I kept my teakettle and went about boiling the water. We wouldn't have use for the actual tea until the water was ready anyway.

While I waited, and to give myself something to do since his stare was making me sweat, I grabbed two coffee mugs from the cabinet. Normally I'd go with teacups, but I didn't want to give myself the wrong cup, so I made sure his would be the snarky *I don't do mornings* mug, while mine had a cute kitten on it.

He thrummed his fingers on the kitchen island and watched me. Never letting me out of his sight.

I leaned against the counter once I'd done everything I could without looking ridiculous. If he didn't leave the room or get distracted, my plan would fail. Ethan's safety would be up to the werewolves, who might never find him. Even if I scried for him myself, I couldn't go alone in my condition.

Selene leaning into me flashed through my mind. She was the last person I wanted helping me after what Jessa had said about her, but if the werewolves didn't let me in, then I'd be forced to seek her out.

Jessa was currently out of commission, and she'd proven her hatred for werewolves already. She wouldn't help me track him down.

Chad was my only hope.

"Seems you need some of the tea too." Chad's low, rumbling voice made me nearly jump out of my skin. "We'll find him. You just sit back and let us take care of it." He made it sound so easy, like my heart had no reason to break at the fact Ethan could be hurt or dead.

I turned away from him, staring out the kitchen window. "How can you be so sure?"

"Stop—" An unfamiliar ringtone interrupted his words, and I glanced over my shoulder at him. "I need to take this. Stay here." He narrowed his gaze at me and headed into the living room before answering the call.

My breath nearly burst from my lungs in relief. I had no idea how long he'd be gone, so I needed to act quickly before he returned. The teakettle whistled, and I cut the heat to it, curious about the guttural murmurings and sizzling energy pulsing from the angry werewolf.

The conversation wasn't going well. Did he have news about Ethan?

"Father, I'm on my way there now. No, I'm not screwing around." He huffed, stomping back into the kitchen.

Keeping my back to him, I slipped several drops of the potion into his cup, put the teabag in, and poured hot water into the mug. I shoved the vial behind the teakettle, hoping he wouldn't notice. The situation balanced on a thin edge, especially with him now so angry.

I turned around and set the tea in front of him as he shoved the phone back into his jeans. He stared down at it with a hint of longing in his eyes. "I don't know if I can. I need to go. I've stayed too long as it is."

My eyes widened, and I nibbled on my lower lip. "You should at least have a taste after I went through the effort of making it, especially with all the tension radiating from you."

However, the tea was boiling hot. Not even I would be able to sip it down right away. Just because he was a werewolf with the ability to heal quickly didn't mean he'd want to scald his mouth. "I could get you some ice?" I smiled doing my best to look encouraging but not too pushy.

"Fine. I'll take some ice, but once I'm done, I'm out of here." He resumed his seat at the island in the kitchen while I put ice in a cup for him to choose as many or as few ice cubes as he wanted. Instead of using ice, I blew on my own tea. I didn't want to dilute the flavor. Besides, I had a feeling I wouldn't have time to appreciate it.

The ice cubes melted almost as soon as they reached the tea, and Chad took a few sips. He blew out a breath, and the lines etched in the corners of his mouth and eyes faded. Soon the whole cup was empty.

I blinked at him, unable to believe he'd guzzled it down. That wasn't how tea should be enjoyed.

He pushed to his feet and gave me a nod. "Thanks. That was just what I needed. I feel better already."

"That's great to hear." I rose and grabbed the crutches. Usually the agreeability potion took ten to twenty minutes to take effect, but I didn't have that time. "We need to get to the Pack meeting now."

Chad met my gaze. The confusion in his eyes shifted to acknowledgement. "Yeah, let's go."

My heart soared. It had worked. Now to figure out how I'd handle the rest of the wolves when we arrived.

15

ETHAN

The research facility loomed behind me with spotlights scanning the area and men everywhere. If anyone tried to get in or out of this place, they'd be detected instantly. My instincts shouted at me that this could be where Jacob and his friend were, but I didn't see how they could have escaped, especially since the security had been beefed up.

My post was on the opposite side from the road close to the woods. Something about this didn't feel right. While everything the military had drilled into me grounded me, the beast yearned to explore and confirm his suspicions.

No way.

Going off half-cocked in this place was perilous. I would be screwed. The mercenaries outnumbered the soldiers around here. The person in charge might not trust us, but they needed the extra manpower we provided.

I kept my gaze on the forest surrounding the massive structure, remaining aware of what potential dangers lurked out there. However, I couldn't quite comprehend why they had this much security. The briefing had mentioned they merely needed to protect the building from terrorist threats.

They were out in the middle of nowhere. Seeing the large and well-guarded building, I couldn't imagine anyone barging in whom the mercs couldn't handle. Besides, if they were some kind of research facility, why did the place have a prison-like feel to it?

I glanced over my shoulder at the actual building and took a deep breath. The only scents I picked up were of the pine trees, vegetation and a few rabbits in the vicinity.

They weren't so much as worried about someone entering this place as much as about someone escaping. The puzzle pieces fit together, and I grimaced, not happy we were a part of this.

My jaw clenched a little and I scratched the back of my neck. The men in Shane's voicemail had sounded like mercenaries recovering the escaped werewolf and his companion. This had to be the place. Before I could bring my wolf back under control, he and I were headed toward one of the side entrances.

I grimaced, holding back my arm as the wolf beckoned me to open it. To my surprise, the door opened and I ducked out of the way as Baldie, the silent mercenary, from earlier walked out. He narrowed his angry eyes at me, but he didn't talk.

What did I say? I'd left my post without permission due to my reckless inner wolf. "Sir, I was looking for a restroom."

He nodded and waved a hand for me to follow him. We walked a few steps, but my hands were wrenched away from my sides and my rifle was taken away. Mercenaries surrounded me, and I hadn't even heard them approach.

What the hell? Shock rocketed through me that they were doing this. The men pulled me down a hallway as if I were a prisoner being brought to a cell. No, this couldn't be happening. *Shit!*

Mia had counted on me to pick her up after work. Now I wouldn't even be able to call her. They couldn't hold me forever, I hoped, but if I showed my true strength, they would know I was a werewolf, and not just a wayward soldier on the way to the restroom.

"What's going on here?" a man in a lab coat hissed. He walked down one of the adjoining hallways. When he had a better look at me and the men clutching me, he threw his hands in the air. "Heaven help me. Can't anything go right here? What is the meaning of this, soldier?"

"Sir, I was only searching for a bathroom." I held myself at attention, which was hard with the mercs holding my arms.

"You shouldn't have come in here." The scientist sighed. "You were strictly briefed before you arrived here. Did you not pay attention?" He nodded to Baldie.

I had no good counter. I did know we weren't supposed to leave our posts. Anyone with half a brain knew that. My idiot wolf had royally screwed things over for us.

If I made it out of here alive, I would spend time with Chad figuring out how to control my urges. My anger and resentment had encroached on our time previously, but now those emotions were gone. What I cared most about was survival and seeing Mia again.

The men shoved me down the hall with Baldie leading the way. They didn't have their guns pointed at me, but there were enough of them to know I wouldn't make it out unscathed if I tried to fight.

A female's agitated cries rang out from somewhere deeper in the labyrinth of hallways. My gut clenched in fear for her. What was going on in this place? We took a few more twists and turns, traveling ever closer.

The woman had long unwashed brown hair. Even

through the hospital gown, I could tell she was too skinny. Something wild shone about her that reminded me of the werewolves I'd seen at the Pack meeting.

I wanted to help, but I'd screwed that up.

She froze in her full-blown thrashing when she saw me. She blinked as if I was some kind of ghost. How long had she been here? "Jacob." The name slipped from her lips in a whisper, but it punched me in the chest. I'd been right.

My heart broke seeing the female in such poor condition, and I knew who Jacob had been protecting. It was *her*.

"What's going on here?" I asked, tugging at my arms. The men at my sides didn't budge. I could break away from them, but now I had a reason not to run. I wanted to help these people. However, if I was locked in with them, we were all in trouble.

Mia and the Pack would never know where to find me, and I would add to the casualty list of whatever experimentation they were doing here.

"Shut your mouth, soldier. You should've stayed at your post." The merc beside me did his best to keep stride with Baldie, but we stopped, waiting for the feral female to be hauled off down the hallway.

She resumed her fierce struggles, but her fight was unorganized as if she was in some kind of drugged haze.

I clenched my jaw and squeezed my hands into fists. They had no compassion for human life here.

The merc on my left side nudged me a little to get me moving again. "She's not what you think. She's dangerous. We're doing the world a favor."

"Jed, keep your lips sealed, or you're going to be sharing a cell with him," the rude merc tossed at the other guy.

I shook my head, irritated with all of them. "You guys are crazy. The military will see that I'm not back at the off-site location. They'll ask questions."

"And we will tell them their soldier disobeyed a direct order."

I closed my mouth, not even willing to waste any more words on them. They were right, which was the worst part about all of this. Damn it.

Baldie glanced back at us as if he was bored of all the conversation, then he unlocked a door to our left. The room held a large cage with a small cot, a bucket in the corner, and that was it. Home sweet home.

Fuck. This was the stupidest thing I'd ever done.

The cage door was already open, as if they were expecting to put someone in there. Unfortunately, that just so happened to be me. Faint scents caught my attention: fear, urine and blood. I cringed, not wanting to go into the cage. For a moment, I didn't care how strong they thought I was.

The ventilation drew away any other smells and the low hum of the air conditioning prevented me from hearing too much else of what was happening within the building, which was pretty odd. If there were a bunch of shapeshifters, I would've imagined I might be able to sense them, but then again, I wouldn't be a full-blown werewolf until tomorrow.

Dread and a cool bead of sweat snaked down my spine. I prayed the werewolves or Mia had figured out my disappearance, because I had a day before the mercs and the scientist realized just how good a catch I'd been.

16

MIA

C had led the way into the Pack Alpha's elaborate mansion. My eyes nearly bugged out when I saw the size and scope of this place. I had assumed they might be in some shack out in the middle of the woods, but not this. From the way Chad dressed and acted, I never would have guessed he'd grown up in the lap of luxury.

Thankfully, the tea had worked wonders, even though time was running out. Werewolves metabolized faster, so he could come to his senses at any moment. I was still impressed with my magical talents, though.

Chad carried my large bag that barely passed as a purse. It held everything I'd need to scry for Ethan's location, granted the werewolves hadn't found him already, which I hoped against hope they had.

Jessa's potion had worked to the point where I didn't need the crutches, but they were still preferred. This was ridiculous. How would I be able to help? I bemoaned my injury, wishing we'd just told my family about our relationship in the first place.

Nolan would have a serious hissy fit over it, but he

needed to realize that Ethan and I were adults. We had our own lives and we wanted to live them out together.

First I needed to convince the Pack of that. Even if I found Ethan, they couldn't believe they had a monopoly over our future. He should be with me, and not with a female werewolf who wouldn't love him nearly as much as I did.

Perhaps by helping with this, they might realize my potential. I only hoped that didn't mean biting me and making me one of them. But if what I'd heard was right they wouldn't stoop that low, since the Alpha didn't want new werewolves to be made.

Chad held the door to what looked like a conference room open for me. Several men and a couple women stared and glanced between Chad and me. One man in particular leapt to his feet. He slammed a fist on the massive oak table and watched us with wild eyes. "What is the meaning of this, Chad?"

"She asked to come to the meeting. She can help find them." Chad didn't sound like his former grouchy self; instead, he appeared oblivious to the severity of the werewolves' reactions.

I remained behind him, hoping he would protect me if someone attacked. Fear gathered in my throat, threatening to cut off my air, but I shoved it down, knowing I would look weak in front of the werewolves who had been contemplating killing my boyfriend.

That thought sent anger burning inside me, renewing my strength. I stood a little taller, or as much as I could on crutches, and assessed the group. I kept my eyes at a level where they'd know I wasn't challenging them, but not low enough that they thought I was completely docile.

"That's the witch who nearly killed our Alpha, isn't it?" one of the wolf men shouted in rage and surprise. A greying pencil thin mustache lined his upper lip and he was seated a few spots away from their leader, meaning he had to have influence in the Pack.

"I am standing right here." I took a step to left so I stood beside and a little behind Chad.

"That doesn't matter. What matters are your crimes against our Alpha." This man was dressed in a black suit and had sleek blond hair. He darted toward us, reaching for me. "You should be punished for your actions."

Chad blocked the blond man with ease. "Get away from her. We both..." He waved to the rest of the room. "We all know this witch crafted the salve that nearly killed my father, our Alpha. However, she didn't realize what she was doing." My eyes widened. I couldn't believe he was sticking up for me. "When I came to her to fix what she'd done, she readily agreed to concoct the remedy for me. We can't fault her solely on what Jared forced her to do for him. He's the true villain." He pushed the other werewolf back a few steps, nearly making the sleek blond man fall.

I remained in place, unwilling to move or even breathe. With these crutches, I was useless at running, so why did I think coming here was such a grand idea again? That's right... to save Ethan.

"Jared *was* the one who ordered the salve, but if she hadn't created it, we wouldn't have had the problem," the man with the mustache piped up. The other wolves spoke in hushed tones, as if unsure which side to choose.

"Are you going to listen to the excuses from these men, Father?" Chad took a step toward the long conference table where everyone sat, except the Alpha who stood at the head of the table. His chair lay on its side after he stood so quickly.

The Alpha snarled. "You can't expect me to believe you want my thanks for bringing in a human...no...a witch to our meeting?" Before I could comprehend what was going on,

Chad was sailing across the room, then he smacked into a wall.

The distraction prevented me from defending for myself from the impending attack. A hand clenched my throat and I was slammed back against the door. My feet dangled several inches in the air.

The Alpha stood before me, his eyes cold and calculating. He inspected me like prey.

I clasped my hands over the Alpha's, struggling for air. What had I been thinking? Barging into the Pack's meeting like this had been crazy. Now I'd die, and Ethan would remain in danger.

I only hoped he'd release me and realize I could help. Jessa had agreed I'd make the salve for Jared on her behalf. I hadn't known what I was getting into. If there was anything I could go back and fix in my life, that would be it.

While changing that event might mean not being with Ethan, I knew he would've been safe and not turning furry once a month. Also, the group of werewolves wouldn't have known I existed, so they wouldn't want me dead because I'd had a lapse of bad judgment and been suckered into doing something because of my mentor.

The Alpha didn't look like he was going to let me go. I wanted to use my magic on him, but I couldn't breathe, let alone whisper the words necessary to protect myself.

"Father, let her go." Chad stood, but he didn't come any closer. Blood trailed down his cheek from an open gash. I couldn't believe how bad the cut was, but his father was a werewolf who could put a lot of force into his punches. Now I knew why Chad hadn't spoken so well of his father before.

He respected the man, but his father wasn't the type who listened to what others thought. There were probably others in the Pack who stroked his ego even further. Maybe some of the wolves who had worked with Jared were here. Could that be why Jessa hadn't received justice yet?

Black spots marred my vision, and my body grew heavier. I wished I could speak to cast my magic. Maybe that was why the Alpha had me by the throat. I tried to whisper the words, but I didn't feel the slow build of magic inside me. My lungs burned with the need to breathe.

The Alpha frowned at me, considering me closer. "What are you trying to say, girl?" He released me, and I dropped to the ground like a sack of flour.

My injured foot hit and I bit back a scream. No, they wouldn't get the pleasure of seeing me in pain like this. I sucked in a deep breath, then whispered a spell under my breath. While normally I might cast protection, I was far too upset to do that. I'd rather error on the side of aggression if they weren't going to take me seriously.

Within moments, a fireball brightly burned in my palm. Heat scalded my hand, but I didn't care. I wanted to throw the fireball at the Alpha, but I held it between us like a shield.

"Witch, put it away." Chad inched closer to me as if afraid I'd turn it on him. "You don't want to do this." I was grateful he was now considering helping me; however, it was a little late. His father didn't back off, instead he watched me as if he didn't believe I'd do anything.

There was no way I'd get out of this alive with the way things were going. I wanted to just curl into a ball, but I'd come here with a mission. I wouldn't let these werewolves ruin that. "You need my help. I can help find Ethan."

A low rumble of voices came from the people still sitting at the table taking in our spectacle. Wasn't that great? They thought we were some kind of entertainment for them. If I'd been braver, I would have screamed at them.

"How would you hope to accomplish that when some of my best trackers haven't been able to establish a location for our missing?" One of the female werewolves spoke up from the table. She was tall, blond, and looked bored by the whole thing as if we were wasting her time.

"The..." My throat cracked as I tried to talk and I cleared it to try again. "The same way I would do anything. Magic. I have my tricks. You need me."

The female werewolf sighed. "We don't need you, but if you're the best hope for finding my son, then we should consider accepting her help, Alpha."

I blinked, not expecting to hear that. Her son? What had I stumbled into?

"Fine. Show us your magic tricks. Help find them, but then you're out of here, and that's for your own good. If we see you around here again, you're dead, witch." The Alpha walked back to the head of the table.

Now was as good a time as any when I had some semblance of power. The woman wanted to find her son, and she'd talked the Alpha into having me help, so that meant they weren't able to find him on their own. If that were the case, I might be allowed have Ethan, instead of him mating with a female werewolf.

Chad touched my arm and I looked over at him. He shook his head as if he knew what was going through my thoughts, but I couldn't just sit back and not try.

"That's not good enough," I said, surprising myself at my boldness. "If I help you find her son and Ethan, then I want you to acknowledge that Ethan is *my*... mate... my boyfriend."

The Alpha growled and marched toward me. "You are a stubborn and stupid girl. Don't think you can push to have your own way here. My word is law."

"Father, they already have a relationship—"

The fireball still burned in my palm, and if I didn't want to seriously injure myself, I needed to extinguish it or throw it. The Alpha was making that decision much easier by the minute.

"Silence!" The Alpha loomed over us as if he thought we could be threatened so easily.

Chad shrank back a little.

Well, at least one of us could be threatened. However, I had nothing to lose here. If I couldn't be with Ethan, then it was like death. I couldn't imagine going back to the kind of abusive relationship I'd been in with Greg, and he was more than willing to take me back.

"If I can get my son back, then give her what she wants. That boy wasn't born a wolf. It doesn't matter if he's mated to a female werewolf. Jacob was. Do you think it's better to not have her assistance in finding our missing, or caving in to the witch's one demand?" The mother werewolf leaned forward at the table. The nonchalant and uncaring look on her face had disappeared. She looked like a woman willing to do whatever it took to get her child back. "Besides, I'd rather have my boy mated with a female wolf. A wolf born as a wolf. Don't you agree?" She narrowed her eyes at the Alpha. The others around her nodded their agreement.

The Alpha slammed a fist on the table, not happy to be challenged, and the group quieted down. "Fine, but you will die if you don't find them. You won't walk out the front door."

The fireball flickered out in my hand and my palm was bright red with a few blisters forming. My gaze landed on a wall clock. Oh, shit. The tea was starting to wear off now.

Chad tightened his grip on my arm and he watched me with a new look in his eyes. The normal Chad was back, not the man who had protected me. He opened his mouth to say something, then he stopped.

"I will find them." I lowered my gaze a little, feeling very uncomfortable with all of the tension in the room. I couldn't let my fear overcome my abilities as a witch. If I did, then I might as well be dead, because that's what would happen.

"You better," the female werewolf said.

The Alpha nodded. "Take her away. She should get started on her 'magic tricks' right away."

I gulped.

Chad pulled me with him, grabbing the crutches and my purse on his way out. I could barely keep up with him hopping and that made me hurt more.

"Slow down. Please."

Only when we were in a different part of the house or should I say mansion, did he finally stop, shoving me away from him.

I gripped a wall to keep from falling.

"You used me. You put something in that tea." His face scrunched up with anger. "You have no idea what you've done. You think you can come in here and fling your magic around like you're hot shit, but you're only putting yourself in danger. You may think my father won't kill you, but you're disposable to them." He wrenched open the door to my right, grabbed my upper arm and pushed me into the room. "Get busy."

17

MIA

*N*ight had descended, and I sat in the back of the car. I'd been able to get a general location by scrying a map of the area, but I'd had to come along to get something clearer since I didn't think a fifty mile radius was exactly what we needed right now. The werewolves had obliged... barely.

Chad was glued to my side as both my pseudo protector and one of the main people holding a big grudge against me. I shrank away from him and the incredible power that billowed around him like an angry wind.

The other werewolves in the car weren't thrilled about my presence either, but I think some of the problems with their emotions were due to Chad giving off so much negative energy.

I elbowed him softly. "Calm down. You're affecting my magic."

Instead of turning to me or saying anything smart, which I had highly anticipated him doing, he just took a deep breath and looked out the side window. Within moments, the atmosphere in the car was a lot more bearable. Even the other wolves grew slightly less agitated. Thank goodness for sensibility.

"Please, stop at the next intersection long enough for me to scry." During the last two, the werewolf had blown through as if we starred in a police drama or action movie and were in hot pursuit of a bad guy that didn't follow traffic signs.

No offense to them, but I wasn't a werewolf. If someone rammed the car as we barreled through an intersection, the werewolves would be just fine. Me on the other hand, I wasn't equipped with their massive healing capabilities.

"Do as she says," Chad grumbled.

They reached the intersection and the car skidded to a stop. My neck jerked forward, then back, and my stomach jolted within me. I almost wished I hadn't mentioned anything, except this was one of the ways scrying worked.

The crystal would lead us to the direction we were meant to go. I held it still for the briefest of moments, since the werewolf driver had caused it to go spinning out of control, then I focused my thoughts on asking where we needed to go.

It swayed side to side. *Go left.* Frowning, I took a deep breath and looked one way, then the other way. "The crystal says left."

The werewolf glanced back at me, as if looking for verification that I wasn't making things up. His gaze locked with the swaying crystal in my hand, then went to my face. But he turned to the left just as I'd requested.

When we came to the next intersection, he stopped again. This time the crystal swayed from the front to the back. "Keep going straight." Very rarely did the crystal want us to turn around, so I was fairly confident in my estimation. However, while I liked to think I was being super useful with scrying, it wasn't something I'd done too much before. I had a long way to go before I could claim mastery.

Mostly I'd played with it when I was younger to ask questions on when I'd meet a boyfriend, or answers on multiple-choice homework. A few times, I may have frustrated my deity since the answers were mostly incorrect. After that, I gave up scrying. Then again, I didn't always have the best relationship with Karma, as noted by the horrible break-up with Greg last month.

I frowned at the way the crystal suddenly started swaying as we passed an old gas station. "Wait. Turn around. I think we found something." I couldn't tell since it was so dark.

The seat beside me groaned as Chad moved. "Do it," he said.

When we got back to the abandoned gas station, the men spread out and knelt low to the ground sniffing. None of them bothered to shapeshift, but it was for the best. I didn't want to see that. While I loved Ethan, seeing a werewolf change into a wolf would probably be more than I could handle.

"They were definitely here." The driver pointed to skid marks bolting from the station that were headed in the direction we'd come.

The passenger sniffed a little closer in a spot away from us. "Jacob's scent lingers over here. Just barely. There's another werewolf with him. Female, I think." He crawled over to another area, sucking in another deep breath. "There were at least three men after them here."

I couldn't help the fascination coursing through me at watching him work. To know I was making a difference made my heart soar. However, we still hadn't found them.

"Looking at the tire tracks, I think our destination will be there." Chad pointed toward the woods. "Jacob must have parked his car here while coming after this mysterious female, and if that's the case, we're not that far." Relief sagged his shoulders, and he glanced in my direction, the faintest bit of respect in his eyes. "Thank you, witch."

I smiled. "I'm happy to help." The other two werewolves stared at me, and nervousness wedged into my chest. "What do we do now?"

"I'm going to call my father and have the other werewolves in the area help us. You're going to wait in the car." Chad nodded his head to the wolf who'd been in the passenger seat, and the wolf stalked toward me.

I bared my teeth at Chad, but hurried back to the car before the wolf could touch me, then rolled down the window to try to hear the phone conversation. The wolf crossed his arms over his chest, keeping watch on me as if I'd make a move to get out of the car. While I didn't want to be in here, there wasn't anything for me to do right this second.

"Father, I have good news. We have a location." Chad beamed. I only hoped he didn't forget who had given them the location. It had taken a lot of my power to concentrate on the crystal, and only now did I realize the strain it had put on my body.

I didn't hear the full response from the other end, but whatever the Alpha told his son, it seemed to please him. A small smile crept onto his lips. "We'll wait for them and check around a little beforehand. I'd like to get this done and over with," he finally said before hanging up.

There must have been a look on my face as he turned toward me. With a shrug, he finally relented his secrets. "We'll be getting some backup. However, I still want you to be out of the way. When the men arrive, tell them we are scouting ahead. The enfor... the guy asking will know what that means," he stated, wolf amber tinting his dark eyes in the moonlit night.

I was too tired and anxious to answer him. After being stuck in the car with three wolves, I needed some space of my own. However, I couldn't help but wonder what would happen if the men in charge of taking the werewolves and Ethan drove by. I slumped further in the seat.

The werewolves took off jogging through the woods, following a trail only visible to their noses. How amazing it must be, truly feeling and sensing the world through more than just their eyes. The trail had been out in the elements for weeks, but they were able to follow with ease.

Yet I wouldn't want their lives. My own magical world was dear to me. With a sigh, I turned and scoured the road, waiting for the rest of the wolves to arrive.

After fifteen minutes, I heard the rumbling engines of several cars. A small convoy pulled into the gas station and parked around the driver's car. Stern faces scanned the woods around me. Here and there, I saw noses flaring. The wolves were eager to hunt.

A broad-shouldered man got out of the first car and lifted his golden eyes to capture mine. There was very little humanity left in them. All I could sense was impending doom for anyone stupid enough to get in his way. There was no question, no words spoken from him. There was no need.

"They headed that way," I said, pointing to where Chad and the two wolves entered the forest. "They are scouting ahead. Chad wanted me to tell you that." I would've continued, but he gave me a sharp nod cutting off further conversation.

"Thanks, witch. Stay here. We will be back soon. No one will be here to hold your hand, so don't move from that car," the brutish man growled before ordering the wolves out.

My thoughts fractured as they departed through the woods, heading to Ethan's location. Glancing up at the sky, the nearly full moon shone down on me. Tomorrow, he would be one of them. Tears burned in my eyes.

As long as he lived. That was all that mattered.

ETHAN

*M*y wolf shook inside my skull, straining against my flesh, wanting to be released. The uncanny feeling had grown stronger by the day.

A pair of fluorescent lights on the ceiling lit my prison. The shades they cast around the room seemed to move and shift around me, making me uneasy. I knew the flashing came from one of the bulbs that would fail soon, but it did little to calm the beast beneath the surface.

Here and there, my mind played tricks on me. I thought I heard noises or smelled things that didn't belong to this part of the country. No wonder the female lurked on the edge of insanity. Suddenly, something drew my attention from my contemplation. The faint clink of metal came from somewhere outside the room. *Had I imagined that too?*

Moments passed and I nearly gave up hope. The general alarm blared to life around me. Something was taking place. First screams of distress and steady gunfire came from the other side of the thick walls around me.

I wanted to shout, give my location, but how would anyone hear me?

The doors along the hallway were torn from the hinges. Metal screeched, coming ever closer to my containment unit. Long trailing claws breached the door, shredding through like it was cardboard. The wolf inside me howled its relief, nearly driving me to my knees, waiting for whoever was coming for me.

The beast's scent hit me. He smelled familiar yet odd. There was a mix of undertones behind the musky layers, namely blood and aggression. Chad had told me about him. The Pack's enforcer was here tearing down the door to get to me.

I grinned. Any hostility I'd had toward the Pack vanished. While I still didn't want to mate with the female werewolf, I owed them a lot for saving my life. My lips quirked in a grin. Both the beast and I knew this was our chance. We would not be constrained. The enforcer nodded his head at me in recognition and made his way to the cage's door.

A few moments of struggle later, he broke the lock and opened the cage. *Free! Run, go!* My brain was spurred on by the primal screams echoing down every hallway. How many shapeshifters had they locked away in this facility? I cringed as dozens of people in hospital gowns and various animal forms ran down the hall with a couple Pack wolves leading the way. My legs took on a life of their own. I had to help out, but the wolf insisted on following the subconscious commands of survival and launched me from the cage towards a flock of shifters in the hallway.

I was fast. Too fast to think and make my own choices. I blew out a breath, releasing my control to the beast and reveling in the freeing sensation of the moment.

A mercenary turned the corner. His gun was aimed low when I kicked him center mass, pinning him on the corner wall. Using his falling body as a surface, I placed my foot on his knee and pounced further out. The sickening pop of his knee giving way would normally have turned my stomach a little, but this was survival. *Do or die.*

Another containment door was visible in the wall, still unbroken by the enforcer. The thought of leaving anyone behind was too much to bear. I made a bee-lined to the door and pulled, unsure if I could tear it apart. Putting my foot against the wall for support, I put my back into it. It groaned but didn't break. A werewolf running by stopped and jerked the door, joining his strength to mine. It popped open, and I nodded to him before heading into the room.

Two figures, a male and a female, stared at me from the cage. It was sturdier than mine, and the locks on it were reinforced. *No simply tearing this open, I guess.* The eyes and underlying scents of the prisoners bore the now familiar tones of werewolves. I recognized the female as the longhaired brunette I'd seen struggling in the hallway earlier. The male must've been Jacob.

The nearby table had various reports and notes, along with multiple vials of blood. I scanned it, finding a forgotten keycard under the latest of scribbled notes taken by a Dr. Peacock. I retrieved it, releasing the two from the cage.

"The research. The vials and everything needs to be destroyed. Listen, it's important. They must have nothing," the blond man said, supporting the woman as they limped out of the cage's door.

I threw the vials into the corner of the room, breaking them. While an imperfect solution, at least the samples would be contaminated. The papers however could be of use to finding out what the scientists wanted. "Don't get rid of them." I stuffed the papers in the woman's arms. "The Alpha should look over what they were after first."

The man narrowed his eyes at me. "You're not even a full-blooded wolf yet. Why should I—"

"Jacob, he's right. Let's just take them and get out of here."

The woman stared adoringly in the male's eyes, and he nodded. "Thank you for helping us."

A feral growl ripped through the hallway making us jump, as we were reminded of the preciously little time we had left before our window of opportunity ran out. *We have to leave.*

The three of us darted into the hallway and ran at full speed in the direction the other wolves had gone. Right around a corner was the faint smell of pine trees. Managing to stop my wolf at the doorway, I glanced into the courtyard.

Here and there, the fence had been torn open, and the sole guard—Horn, by the looks of it—lay on the ground bleeding near me. I froze, torn between the need for freedom and the oath to keep my squad alive. *Shit!*

The searchlight turned in my direction and determination reignited my drive to seek safety. I ran for it, and the couple behind me followed. Semi-automatic gunfire raked the forest floor around us. Whoever was shooting could have used some more time on the firing range. I ducked behind some big rocks and tree trunks, directing the two into safer zones.

A scent trail around us indicated the wolves had come this way, leaving me a clear-cut path to follow where the Pack had arrived. The fresh scent of the forest invigorated me and I eased up a little. *Have we made it?*

The trail was quiet. There was no sign of anyone else. My skin began to crawl. There had been others and the complex wasn't that big. Where was everyone? Nervousness filled me and I let loose the growl building up in my throat before heading along the path again.

Up ahead was a small clearing with an abandoned gas station. My gaze zeroed in on pacing feminine shape. *Mia!* It took me a moment to notice my two companions had ducked farther into the woods. I slowed down. But this was not how it appeared.

First, faintly, then more strongly I smelled them. Gunmetal, nervous sweat and men. They were at the corner of the gas station slowly moving to surround Mia. I watched as they finally made themselves known to her and slammed her face into the ground. *They would not hurt her.*

Without a thought, I ran through the trees separating us, taking advantage of the shadows and the mercenaries' flashlights.

Four of them were in her immediate vicinity, while two others were checking the row of parked cars.

I circled around the gas station and headed to the last car, while a guard was busy looking at the underside of the blue one. When he was done and moved on to check the red car, I punched him in the jaw. His neck snapped back with a sharp crack and he dropped into my arms. I carefully set him down and moved on to the other guard checking the cars. The final two guards in the immediate area were yanked into the shrubbery, and I saw Jacob appear soon after, nodding at me before ducking back out of sight.

While I didn't enjoy hurting them, I had to admit to feeling a sense of satisfaction. Hopefully they wouldn't hurt anyone else anymore.

When I rose from my spot behind the car, the final two guards were escorting Mia back toward the complex. They leaned toward each other, and before long, a telltale flicker of light from a lighter ignited the end of a cigarette. Apparently, the smokers thought it was good time to relax. *Seriously, where do they hire these goons?*

There was little to do now, other than to get to Mia. With a slow and low-to-the-ground run, I was part of the way to them when a twig snapped under my foot.

The guards escorting Mia pointed their guns my way.

I ducked behind the first vehicle as bullets started flying. By the pace they were going, I knew to wait for the reload. The wolf's enhanced hearing told me when the magazines on both guns hit empty. *Gotcha! This is why one lays fire and another waits.*

I broke into run, grabbing a knife from a sheath on the closest body. One of the guns just clicked a magazine in as I flung the knife toward the guard who I believed had been shooting faster. The gun barrel had just begun to rise when it dropped to the ground.

Not losing any time I ducked behind the closest tree, just as the magazine on the other gun hit home. The ground kicked up around me from the impact of the medium caliber bullets. This time the man used two shots at a time, slowly walking backward. He had the advantage, and he knew it now. What he didn't account for was Mia.

I heard an oomph come from the mercenary and I ducked out of my cover. The man was regaining his balance, even as Mia had turned and began to run away. The barrel of his gun pointed toward her, and I cursed under my breath. The merc took deliberate aim, giving me a few precious moments. I couldn't reach Mia in time. We were on opposite sides of the trail. If I ran at him, I'd be in the firing line. To me, the choice was obvious. The wolf leant me all of its strength.

Mate in danger.

I leapt for him with brutal force. The world slowed down as I stared into the eyes of my target. The mercenary noticed me too late. The gun went fired seconds before I knocked the barrel away. His eyes were the size of small saucers. Even as the bullet bit into my chest, I knew I had done my duty. She would be safe.

Pain exploded through me, and a few moments later, I slammed the man who shot me into the ground. His head hit hard on a rock, but he wasn't dead. His breathing was laborious and his eyes wild.

I punched him with all my remaining power before sliding off to his side and looking up at the trees. Blackness crept into my vision and the pain faded a little around the edges. *If only I could see her one more time.*

"Ethan, no!" Mia's sobs were the last thing I heard. Her soft lips the last thing I felt.

MIA

*T*he crazy werewolf driver went to Jessa's home before heading back to the Pack's mansion. Thankfully, Jessa had agreed to come with us, despite the fact she'd be with a group of werewolves. Only with her help could I perform the healing ritual that might very well save Ethan's life, even though he was less than a day from becoming an actual werewolf.

A couple of Pack werewolves brought him into a room that looked like it regularly dealt with these kinds of dire situations. Chad's pale skin and the concern in his eyes proved he wasn't confident Ethan's injury was survivable.

My heart pounded in my chest, nearly shattering my tenuous concentration. I chanted a healing spell under my breath over and over, placing my hands over the area where Ethan had been shot. One of the werewolves confirmed that the bullet had gone clean through, so we didn't have to worry about any pieces remaining inside Ethan.

Jessa chanted with me, but she was also busy setting up candles and lighting incense in preparation. Her gaze shifted to the werewolves gathered around the room who were watching us as if we were about to do a magic trick. Her nostrils flared and her voice trembled. If the gathering didn't leave, she might not be able to assist me with this.

I turned my head in Chad's direction, but he was talking with a thickly accented werewolf, who had on loosely fitting jogging pants and an oversized t-shirt. Shaggy red hair framed his face. "I have to go home to Scotland." His tight shoulders hunched over, but a feral light shone from his brown eyes. "I need to reconnect with my wolf, mate. We're broken."

I couldn't imagine what he'd gone through. What any of them had gone through locked away in the research facility. Most of the werewolves looked like they were ready to snap at any moment.

Chad glanced between me and the Scottish werewolf. "How do I know you won't lose control? I'm not sure my father will want you to leave. We need all the wolves we can get, especially with this attack against us." He sighed, sounding almost helpless. "Fine, I'll talk with him. Take care of yourself, and I want you to check in. The Pack is here for you, Colin. You'll call ahead to the Scottish Pack, right?"

"Not like there are many wolves remaining in that Pack, but, aye, I will." Colin rubbed his forehead as if kneading away some of the tension there. "This isn't permanent. I'll be back." He tilted his head to Chad, then he limped from the room.

Jessa cleared her throat and I jerked my head back in her direction, shocked that I'd been caught up in Chad's conversation with the broken werewolf. She cocked an eyebrow at me. The mentor I trusted stared at me with disapproval in her gaze, not in the least like the shattered victim of a werewolf attack.

"Chad, we need the werewolves out of here. We need to focus." With that said, I joined hands with Jessa over Ethan's body and closed my eyes, giving in to the pull of magic coursing through me down my arms and connecting with the strong torrent of power that sizzled over my wrists and forearms where her palms touched.

Energy grew within the room until it nearly choked me with its potency. If it weren't for Jessa's grip, I might've flopped off the bed. Our voices rose in synchronized cries to the deities pleading for Ethan's recovery. My hands burned with almost a scalding heat, as if I was holding a fireball in my palm for too long. I wanted to open my eyes and see what was happening, but I knew not to break the connection. If I did this might fail, and Ethan could die.

The magic slithering through us reached boiling point, and Jessa forced my palms onto Ethan's bloody chest. My eyes flew open as the power that built between Jessa and me poured through my hands and into Ethan. The sensation was almost too much for me to stand, but her firm grip held me in place.

I met her gaze and she nodded to me, a reassuring smile on her lips. Weariness stole through me, and my body slumped backward. It was everything I could do to keep my eyes open.

Hands held me up and Jessa released me. I glanced back to see Chad. He lowered me beside Ethan, whose breathing was slow and steady. His pale complexion improved before my eyes. I rested my hand on his arm, then closed my eyes.

---

*W*hen I woke up, the sun shone through the windows, bringing in plenty of natural light. The candles and all remnants of the healing ritual were gone, except for the faint scent of sandalwood that lingered in the air.

Slight movement at my side nearly made me jump off the bed.

Ethan squinted up at me. His brilliant blue eyes were a sight to behold. I'd been so afraid of him dying.

Tonight you still might lose him. I shove the thought from my mind. *No.* Whatever happened, we were in this together. We'd been given a second chance, and I refused to throw it away.

The werewolves who'd crammed into the room to watch had been impressed, even if I had been afraid that Jessa might lose her nerves with them all watching. But she was a much stronger witch than me because her concentration was impenetrable.

"Hi, babe," Ethan said, his voice hoarse. He started to sit up on the bed, but I put my hand on his shoulder.

"Hey, honey. How are you feeling?" I leaned in, placing a chaste kiss to his lips. While he'd recovered last night, I slept at his side. If the ritual hadn't drained me, I would've been watching over him. I'm pretty sure I had dark circles under my eyes and my hair was sticking out in all directions.

He opened his mouth to respond but he coughed instead, unable to get the words out.

Chad walked into the room with a cup of water and a straw in his hand. I didn't like being in Werewolf Central, but he'd been a good helper. So much so, that I almost wondered if he'd had more of the agreeability potion.

I helped Ethan take a few sips of water then set it aside, brushing my hand over his short dark hair before he tried to speak again.

"I feel like I got shot in the chest, but I'll live." He wrapped his arm around my waist pulling me close, as Chad settle into a chair on the opposite side of the bed from where I sat. "Why didn't I go to a hospital?"

"You're too close to turning into a werewolf. Besides, the

doctors wouldn't have been able to save you, unlike your girlfriend and her friend." Chad looked in my direction. "Maybe the witches aren't enemies of the Pack after all."

"Thank you, babe." The hard look in Ethan's eyes softened as he met my gaze. "Where was everyone last night?" he asked Chad, sitting up again. This time he shrugged off my attempt to hold him down. "I followed the scent and went to the cars, but no one else was there. Mia was left alone."

Chad grimaced and looked away from him, turning his gaze to the open window. "Several of the prisoners were determined to seek revenge. They burnt the research facility down. We needed to make sure they didn't get hurt, so most of us assisted them."

Ethan clenched his jaw, obviously not pleased with that answer. "I need to get home. My roommate might be worried, and I need to call work to explain my absence." He nudged me aside, then pushed himself out of bed. He swayed on his feet and I rushed to his side, helping him stay upright.

"You should lie down and rest. Don't worry about that. I can call Nolan, and you don't have to go home to call work." I frowned, not wanting him to push himself too hard. While I was pretty sure the magic had been successful, the image of him fading away in my arms still squeezed at my chest. The idea of not being with him to see if he was okay sent my pulse skyrocketing.

"Listen to her. She knows what she's talking about," Chad said, and coming from him that was a compliment of the highest order.

I couldn't suppress the smile springing to my lips.

"I need to get home and make sure Nolan knows I'm fine. The full moon is rising tonight, and my shift into the supernatural world will be complete. I want normalcy before being drawn into that." Ethan pulled me into his arms, but his words still hurt. "Besides, we have something to tell him and your parents. If we can survive me getting shot, we'll survive their reactions."

"You shouldn't go too far, Ethan. Not with tonight being your first shift." Chad rose from the chair. "You'll need assistance, and we have plenty of room to run wild here." He turned to me. "You might not want to be here. It's not for the faint of heart. I'll be back later." He tilted his head, then walked out of the room.

"Are you sure about telling my family?" I met Ethan's gaze. My heart sang in happiness, even if a shiver of fear spread through me. "Especially Nolan? What if he takes things badly?"

"Our relationship might change once I truly become a werewolf tonight. But I believe in us enough to spread the word. No more tiptoeing around your family." He locked his eyes with mine, a knowing look buried in their depths. "We deserve better than that, for better or for worse. Nolan will have to come to terms with the news."

"We can't hide forever," I said, my voice cracking from the mixture of emotions brewing within me. "Not from those closest to us."

"Not anymore, babe." He leaned in, pressing a kiss to my lips, before tugging me backward onto the bed. I couldn't believe he was ready for intimacy after all he'd been through, but then something I'd read in Jessa's werewolf book came back to mind: werewolves were like sex fiends during the full moon.

I only hoped I'd be able to keep up with him...

Ready for more Cry Wolf? Grab the next book in the series, *Highland Moon Rising*...

AUTHOR'S NOTE

Thank you for reading *The Wolf Who Played With Fire*. I hope you enjoyed it!

After writing *Cold Moon Rising*, the plot for this book unfolded in my head piece by piece beckoning me to dive into it. I absolutely enjoyed continuing Mia and Ethan's journey while getting a glimpse at Kelly and Jacob from the outside. Don't fret though since I'll pick back up with Kelly and Jacob. Their story is just beginning.

One of the things I love about this series is it's a lot of fun to write and I love revisiting the characters as well as meeting new ones. The books come together almost effortlessly, which hasn't been the case in the past with other series I've written. If you have a favorite couple you'd love to see in future books, let me know through Instagram, Facebook, or email me!

Please consider leaving a review at the retailer's site or on Goodreads, even if it's a line or two. It truly helps!

Craving more? Get *Hunter's Moon Rising*, a bonus story about a woman who learns she's dating a werewolf here.

ACKNOWLEDGMENTS

I'd like to give a big thank you to my husband who patiently listens to my excited chatter about the people who exist entirely in my head. Also, many thanks go to my editor Tessa for her great input into the book as well as Donna F., Elisa, and Donna H. who kindly beta read for me. Finally, a special thank you goes to my readers for your support and excitement about the Cry Wolf series. You guys make writing books the best job ever.

ABOUT THE AUTHOR

Sarah Mäkelä is a New York Times and USA Today Bestselling New Adult Paranormal Romance Author. If shifters, witches, and vampires tangled up in dark, passionate stories are your thing, you're in the right place. Her books deliver romance with a bite, literally.

When she's not writing, Sarah reads sexy books, watches scary movies with her spouse, dives into magical research, or spoils the pets who rule the house. She's also an avid gamer and a night-light enthusiast because you never know what's lurking in the dark. Whenever she can, she loves traveling to new places, finding inspiration and fueling her imagination along the way.

- a amazon.com/author/sarahmakela
- BB bookbub.com/authors/sarah-makela
- instagram.com/authorsarahmakela
- f facebook.com/authorsarahmakela
- X x.com/sarahmakela
- g goodreads.com/sarahmakela
- pinterest.com/authorsarahmakela

ALSO BY SARAH MÄKELÄ

The Amazon Chronicles Series

(Shifter Romance)

Book 1: Jungle Heat

Book 2: Jungle Fire

Book 3: Jungle Blaze

Book 4: Jungle Burn

The Amazon Chronicles Collection

Hacked Investigations Series

(Futuristic Paranormal Romance)

Book 1: Techno Crazed

Book 2: Savage Bytes

Book 2.5: Internet Dating for Gnomes *

Book 3: Blacklist Rogue

Book 4: Digital Slave

Courts of Light and Dark

(Fantasy Romance)

Book 1: Captivated

Book 2: Surrendered

Standalones

Moonlit Feathers

Captive Moonlight

Vera's Christmas Elf

Made in the USA
Columbia, SC
07 June 2025

59068668R00087